A Piltdownlad Zine Collection
THE OLYMPIC SPIRIT

and
other

stories

by
Kelly
Dessaint

published by
Phony Lid Books
2014

A Phony Lid Paperback Original

With eternal gratitude to Irina.

This collection includes the zines, as they appeared in print:

The Güero Chingón Stories Vol. One
Junior Careers
The Olympic Spirit

© 2011, 2012, 2013, 2014
Kelly Dessaint

ISBN: 978-1-930935-38-9

First Printing, June 2014

phony lid books

PO Box 22974
Oakland, CA 94609
www.phonylid.com

The Olympic Spirit

PILTDOWN LAD No. 8

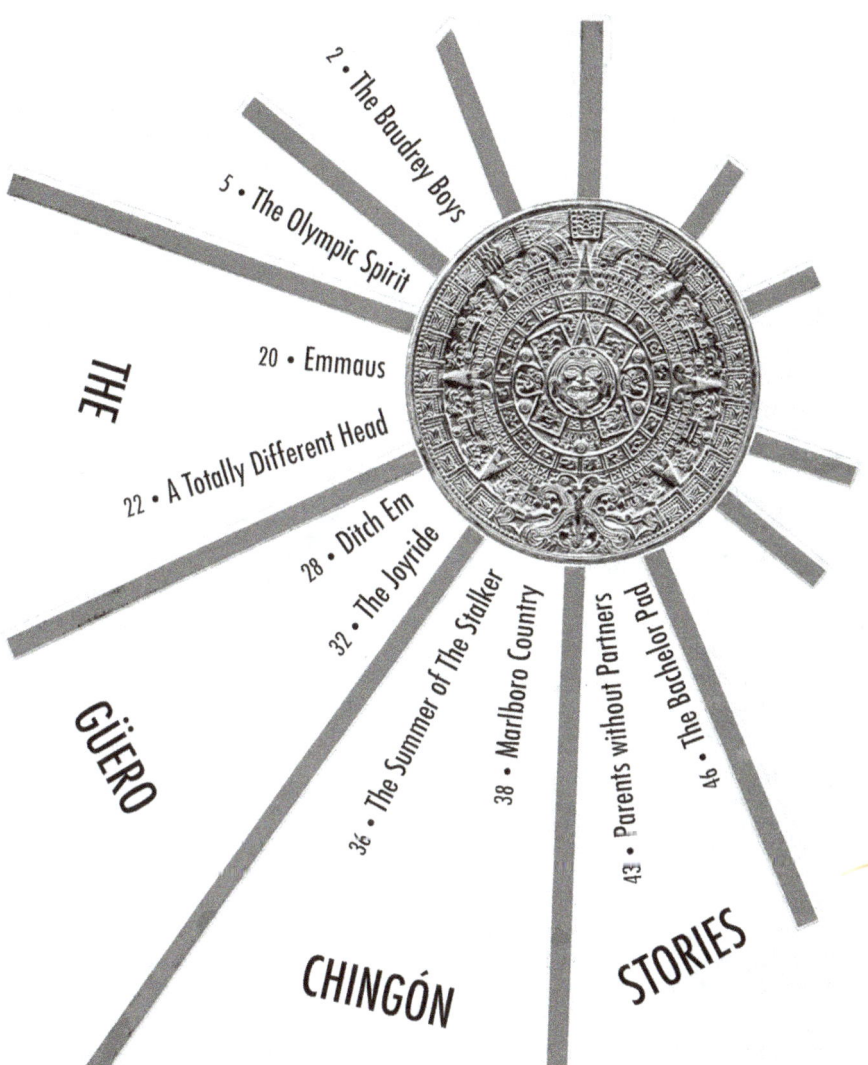

THE GÜERO CHINGÓN STORIES

VOLUME TWO

THE BAUDREY BOYS

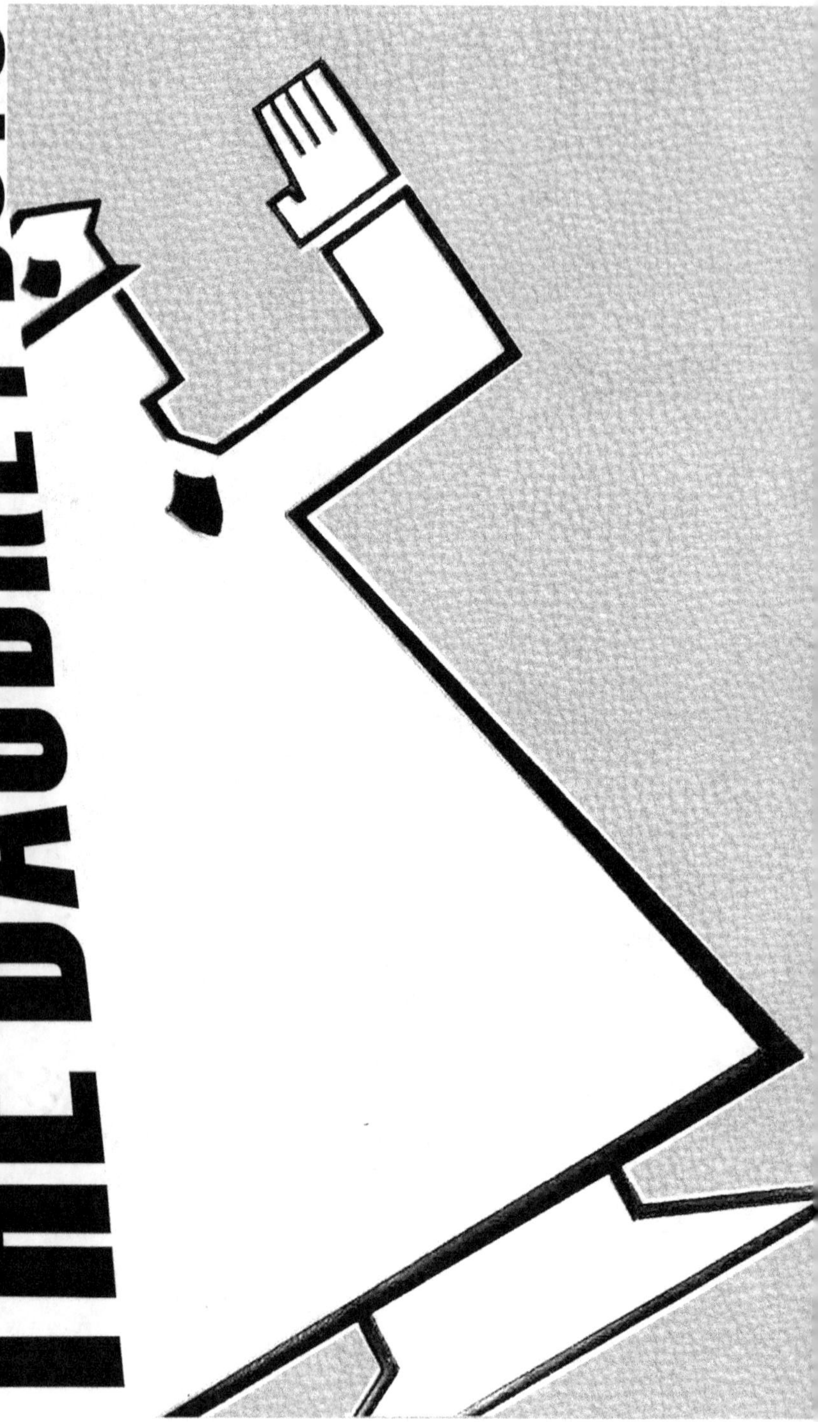

AT THE HOUSE, THERE WERE FIVE OF US. Mom had always
wanted a big family. For fifteen months, Nate was an
only child. Had a good thing going, too, until I showed up and ruined everything. From the moment I entered
the house, the fantasy of a happy family life was shattered. I slipped out of the womb screaming bloody murder. Inconsolable at first sight of the world, I let
out a prolonged wail that lasted three years, until I
could form the proper words to express my disappointment. And even then, I alternated between verbal out-
rage and non-vocal guttural spasms. I was only calm
at bathtime, as if the warm water was a return to the
safety of the womb.

Despite being the second born, my tyrannical behavior
ruled the house. Because I screamed the loudest, my
whims usually came first. Prone to violent rampages,
I avenged any misfortune with cataclysmic fits, running through the house, knocking over furniture and
breaking toys. And then, if that didn't work, crying
until my face looked like a bruise.

The indignities Nate suffered from this unruly addition to his prior peaceful existence were exasperated
even further when Mom started dressing us in identical
outfits. Too close in age for hand-me-downs, and with
dissimilar builds--him, pudgy and me, thin--Mom sim-
plified shopping excursions by purchasing the same item
in different sizes. And since we were the only kids on
the street with blonde hair and blue eyes, we were
often mistaken for twins.

As we got older, Nate and I were quick to point out
that we weren't real brothers. We told people that we
were just cousins, seeing as that we had different
fathers who also happened to be real brothers. This
genetic wrinkle became a point of pride, an opportunity to distance ourselves. After years of
struggling for autonomy, our rivalry was fully solid-
ified when Nate flunked the fifth grade and we ended
up in the same classroom, with only two dozen other
students as a buffer. As soon as we got home, the bat-
tles began. In our seesaw battle of wills, our younger siblings were often caught in the middle.

After I was born, it took the folks another three years before they were ready to risk a third addition to the family. This time they had a girl. Claudia entered the fray as a shock absorber to our constant bickering. By the time Joey showed up, the stage was set. Since he didn't look like the rest of us, with his brown curls and olive complexion--he was the only one of us who looked like our father--we told him he was the mailman's kid.

Ten years separated Nate and Danielle, our baby sister. After that, Mom had her tubes tied and closed up shop.

Nate and I may have hated each other, but when it came to raising hell, we were the best of friends. With Joey yapping at our heels. To be a part of the action, he had to take the same abuse we unleashed on each other. Joey was the pipsqueak, always struggling to keep up. Nate and I were bigshots. Too cool to be hanging out with a little kid. We had no choice, though. Mom told us that if we wanted to run around the neighborhood, we had to stick together, look out for each other, keep each other out of trouble and-- goddamn it!--always come home without leaving anybody behind. She felt the need to emphasize this last part since Nate and I had abandoned Joey once during a family outing to Mt. Wilson. After walking around the woods for several hours, we returned to the campsite just the two of us. When Mom asked, "Where's Joey?" we could only shrug. She went into a tirade: "You better go find your brother!" An hour later, we discovered him at the ranger's station eating an eskimo pie. Having a jolly ole time.

So we stuck together. A pack of hooligans, constantly on the prowl for any trace of excitement, which usually consisted of the one thing we were supposed to avoid: T-R-O-U-B-L-E. As far as we were concerned, public property was there to be destroyed. We shoplifted without thinking twice. Give us a book of matches and we'd burn down your house. We created bedlam and ballyhoo at a moment's whim. But no matter how stealth we were in our chicanery, we always seemed to get busted. It boggled our minds how we could have such rotten luck. Nate called me a jinx. I blamed him for being an asshole. Or Joey for being too slow. We didn't put it together until the old man pointed out, during a drive home from the manager's office at the Alpha-Beta, that since we were the only white kids around, all anybody had to do was say the culprits had blonde hair and the cops would know right where to go. Our house.

THE OLYMPIC

SPIRIT

1.

IT WAS THE SUMMER OF 1984. The Olympics
were in town. Everywhere you looked, ad-
vertisements for the games were plastered
on bus benches, newspaper boxes and bill-
boards. Almost all the commercials on TV
had something to do with the XXIII Olym-
piad. By the time the torch bearer lit
the flame at the Coliseum, the city was
rabid with Olympic fever. My brothers and
I were just as excited, but we didn't
care about the sporting events. What we
were psyched about was the promotional
game at McDonald's called "If The US Wins
You Win."

The concept was simple. The cashiers
handed out game cards free of charge. All
you had to do was ask. On the front of
the cards was a round foil medal that
you scratched off to reveal an Olympic
event. If the US team won the gold medal,
you got a Big Mac. For the silver medal,
you got fries. Bronze, a Coke.

At the time we didn't know much about
politics, but the Soviet Bloc had boy-
cotted the games that year. So the US
team, with very little competition, was
winning most of the medals. Which meant
lots of free McDonald's for us.

We ate at McDonald's every day. Each morning we walked the five and a half blocks to the McDonald's on Garvey Avenue to redeem our winning cards and get new ones. In the lobby, they'd set up a board with results of all the events. If we were lucky, we got a card for an event that had already been played. That was like an instant winner. Otherwise, we'd add the game card to our collection and wait.

McDonald's was the holy grail of fast food. I used to dream about eating McDonald's cheeseburgers and fries, only to wake up disappointed that it was just a figment of my imagination. In my subconscious, the McDonald's experience was intensely detailed. From the plastic tray we carried to the table, to the swivel chairs, to the waxy cup of Coke, to the paper sleeve that held the fries.

It was the greatest summer of our lives.

Until the day everything changed. A day like any other. We were on our way to McDonald's, our pockets full of winning cards after the US team kicked some serious ass in track and field, when we passed our old school, Emerson Elementary. Nate stopped and pointed at something through the squares of chainlink.

"You see all that shit in the dumpsters?"

I followed the aim of his finger and noticed they were stuffed with paper and boxes. Pieces of furniture were hanging over the sides.

"Bet there's some cool shit in there," Nate said.

Even though I was craving a McDonald's fix, it was hard to resist a dumpster dive. You never knew what you'd find in the trash. Once, we were scrounging through some junk behind Garvey Junio High and scored a wallet. There was no money inside, just a driver's license and some family photos. But we gave it to Mom and she looked up the guy in the phonebook. Later that evening, a man showed up at the house to retrieve it. Told us some Mexican guys had jumped him in the park- lot at Boy's market. Gave us each a dollar as reward.

Without hesitation, we scaled the fence. By the time Nate had boosted Joey up and over, I was already in- side the dumpster, sifting through the junk and toss- ing the useless stuff onto the asphalt. There wasn't much worth bothering with. So I jumped out and headed towards the buildings.

"Hey, where are you going?" Nate called after me.

"Gonna see my old classrooms."

I crossed the blacktop and went up a flight of stairs to an open walkway that wrapped around a grassy courtyard, where most of the classrooms were. As I walked down the hallway, I looked in the windows and checkled the handles on the doors to see if any were

unlocked, thinking it would have been hilarious to
sit in one of my old desks.

I hated going to Emerson.

From the first day of school, we weren't just
bullied, we were brutalized. With my babyface and
big mouth, I was such a target of contempt, I had
to start running fifteen seconds before the final
bell just to make it out the door without a fare-
well knuckle sandwich. It got so bad, our folks sent
us to the Y to learn karate. But the classes were on
Friday nights, same time as Dukes of Hazard and
Dallas. I didn't see why I had to miss my favorite
TV shows on account of some assholes who didn't like
me because I was born with such loathsome features
as blond hair and blue eyes. Besides, I wasn't much
of a fighter. Self-defense wasn't my thing. So I
learned to run faster. And talked shit like there
was no tomorrow.

After a particularly violent beatdown, when some
kids knocked me off the jungle gym and stomped my
balls until I went into convulsions (if I ever have
kids and they come out deformed, I'll know who to
blame), the folks finagled a way to send us all to
a school in Alhambra.

This was the first time I'd been back to Emerson since
then. I was fun exploring the place when it was empty.

It felt safer.

At the far end of the hallway, there was a room
without a window. I turned the handle and, to my
surprise, it opened. I called Nate and Joey over and
went inside to investigate.

It was a supply room. On the shelves were plastic
binders, construction paper in various colors, pads
of that brown paper with wide lines and dashes down
the center for practicing your handwriting. There
were countless boxes of paperclips, thumbtacks and
rubber bands, as well as boxes of chalk and a pile
of dusty erasers. In one corner, maps were
rolled up. One shelf had nothing but stacks and stacks
of textbooks. I opened a cabinet and inside were
more office supplies and several tubs of finger paint.

"Jackpot!" Nate shouted from across the room. He
held up a box of markers. Magic markers. "There's a
bunch in here." Nate dropped several boxes on a table.
"Pens too!"

Nate and I grabbed all the markers and Joey picked
up the pens.

"Alright, let's get outa here," Nate said. "Before
someone shows up."

We jumped back over the fence and headed down
Stephens. We crossed the street when we passed the
house with the evil bush. They said the devil lived

7

in that bush and if you passed it on the same side of
the street, you'd get fifty years bad luck. Way worse
than stepping on a crack and just breaking your mom's
back.

On the corner of Hellman, next to the mental hospital, we saw Greg, Rick's older brother. They lived
up the street from us. Rick was our friend, but Greg
was practically an adult. He went to Keppel.

We tried to act normal. Said hello.

"What you got there?" Greg pointed at the boxes in
our hands.

Nate did the talking. "Oh, we found these markers
in the trash at Emerson, with all the stuff they were
throwing away."

Greg raised his eyebrows. "You found them?"

"Yeah, in the dumpster. Crazy, huh?"

"Huh. Those markers are good for drawing."

Greg was an artist. Rick used to show us his stuff
all the time, bragging on his brothers like always.
But Greg did some badass shit. He once turned a Pee-
Chee inside out and drew the members of KISS so
perfect, the faces looked the same as the album covers.

"So, what are you gonna do with them?" he asked.

We shrugged.

"If you wanted to sell some, I'd buy them."

"You wanna buy these?" Nate asked, incredulously.

"Sure, however many you don't want."

"You can have them all!"

"Okay. How many you got?"

We put all the boxes together and counted. "Five.
Three black and two red."

"How much you want for them?"

We shrugged.

Greg laughed. "Let's see how much fedya I got on me."

Greg slipped his hand into his pocket and pulled out
a folded bill with a visible five.

We gasped. That was a lot of money.

Greg unfolded the five, looked at it a few seconds
and then handed it to Nate.

"Buck a box?"

"Deal!"

Nate pocketed the cash. We grabbed the pens and took
off down the street. In case Greg changed his mind.

Five dollars!

We were rich!

As we walked home to stash the pens, I tried to figure out how much candy I could buy at the corner store
with my cut. Licorice sticks were three cents each,
chocolate footballs were a nickel a pop... But what
was a third of five? I wasn't that good at math. The
closest I could figure was a buck seventy five each.

8

Six dollars would have been easier on the split, but we only had five boxes.

Then it hit me.

"Hey, I bet there are more markers in the room," I said, full of enthusiastic vigor. "We should go back and get the rest. We can make more money. More money means more candy!"

The only thing better than McDonald's was candy.

"I dunno." Nate was hesitant, just to spite me, no doubt, for coming up with such a brilliant idea.

"Too risky," he said.

"C'mon. Don't be chickenshit."

"Fuck off. I just don't wanna get busted again. Remember Alpha Beta? It was you who wanted to go back the second time. That's why we got caught."

"Ah, that was just bum luck."

"No, you're a jinx."

"Don't be like that. Joey, you wanna go back, dontcha don't you?"

Joey looked at me and the Nate. "Yeah?"

"See, two againt one?"

Still, Nate resisted. But I kept working on him for the rest of the day.

After we hit McDonald's and redeemed our winning cards, we stopped by the corner store for dessert.

That night, as we quietly scarfed the junk food we'd hidden under our blankets, Nate finally caved.

"I guess we can check it out tomorrow."

I knew he couldn't deny that it was the best scheme ever.

2.

It was high noon when we returned to Emerson after our daily transaction at McDonald's. The sun was beating down full blast, like a distorted radio. We stood outside the fence for a while, making sure nobody was around. Nate didn't want to push our luck, thinking that a school offical might be around, and that's why the door was unlocked. But everything looked the same as it had the day before. The tetherball poles glistened in the bright light. The blacktop looked like a sea of tar.

I rattled the ice in my McDonald's cup and slurped the last drop of free Coke, courtesy of our boys who won medals at the discuss throw. With just one event, I scored fries and a Coke. I tossed the cup over the fence and it exploded on the asphalt, echoing off the sides of the buildings.

"Fucker!" Nate punched me in the arm.

"Lay off!" I snapped. "I'm just seeing if the coast is clear."

Sure enough, nothing stirred. So we jumped the fence. When we got to the supply room, the door was still unlocked. We searched the cabinets. But no markers. We looked through the boxes on the shelves. No markers. We dug through the contents of a desk. Still no markers.

"I told you we got them all," Nate said.

"Maybe we can sell some of this other stuff," Joey suggested.

"Who'd want this crap?" I picked up a box of paperclips and chucked it against the wall. Shrapnel went all over the floor.

"Hold up!" Nate was rummaging in the back of the cabinet. "Check it out! Colored pencils."

"You think Greg will buy them?"

"I don't care," Nate said. "I'll take them."

I grabbed a stapler and a ruler. "I could probably use some of this stuff." I charged at Joey with the ruler. "On guard!" Since I had a McDonald's game piece for a fencing event, I'd watched a bout the night before. Seemed like a pretty cool sport. I practiced a few jabs while Joey defended himself with a ring binder.

"Stop fucking around," Nate hissed. "Joey, get those box lids so we can carry this stuff home."

"Hold on," I said. "I'm not finished yet." I plowed a stack of paper onto the floor.

"Oh, no," Nate groaned.

"Oh yeah!" I shoved more paper and boxes off the shelves. Giggling lika a maniac, I unzipped my pants. And then, "It's raining, it's pouring." All over the pile of junk. "Weeeeeeee!"

I dared Joey to take a dump on the floor.

"But I don't hafta go."

I was about to call him a pussy when I remembered the finger paint in the cabinet. I reached in and pulled out a tub. Red like ketchup. "Shotput!" I threw "Shotput!"

The tub of paint hit the wall and the shelves collapsed into an avalanche of paper, wood and paint.

Joey grabbed a tub of blue and chucked it at the other wall of shelves. More paint and wood went everywhere.

"Your turn." I handed Nate a tub of orange.

"Fuck that. I'm outa here."

I made a chicken sound and lobbed the paint into the air. It hit the floor like an atom bomb. Paint splattered onto the ceiling and spread out across the room.

Nate grabbed his box. "See ya suckers later."

When he pushed the door open, sunlight poured into the room, exposing the rainbow of paint, the wads of paper and broken shelves.

"I love what you've done with the place," I told Joey. I picked up my box and followed Nate. I slammed the door behind me and held the handle.

"Let me out!" Joey yelled from the other side, twisting the knob and banging against the door.

Nate cuffed my shoulder. "Let him out, asshole."

He gave me that look, like I was supposed to be scared or something.

"Okay." I let the doorknob go and stepped out of the way.

With all his strength againt it, Joey pushed the door open and it slammed against the stucco wall. A loud thud echoed down the hallway.

"I swear," Nate seethed. "You're the biggest idiot ever. Let's get the fuck outa here. Now!"

"Whatever you say, hoss."

At the end of the hallway, we stopped and looked around. Everything was still calm.

As we walked briskly towards the fence, I saw three guys in the playground.

"Oh shit! We got company."

"Just kepp going," Nate said.

We picked up our pace.

"Hey!"

We'd been spotted.

I looked over my shoulder. The guys were heading our way.

"Hey!"

We pretended we didn't hear them and kept moving.

"Hold up!"

Their voices were getting louder. They were only a few yards away. We'd never make it over the fence without getting caught.

"Let's just see what they want," said Nate.

"Que pasa, güeros?"

The biggest guy spoke first. He had a wicked grin. And his face was greasy, like he'd just eaten a Big Mac and forgot to use a napkin.

"Us? We're not doing anything."

"Sounds like you vatos was up to something." He looked to the guy on his left and asked, "Watcha think, Javie? That sound like nothing to you?"

Javie had a mouth full of snaggled teeth. He was holding a blue and yellow Nerf football with the points chewed off. As he moved it from one hand to the other, I wondered if he had a dog or had chewed the ball up himself.

12

"That definitely sounded like something to me,
Eddie," Javie said.

"What about you, Oscar?" Eddie asked the guy on his
right.

Oscar was holding a McDonald's bag. He smiled with
his eyes half closed, like he was still in the middle of a dream. About food, probably, I thought,
judging by the fat rolls on his neck.

"Simon," Oscar said with a snicker. "These güeros
was up to some shit, for sure."

"What you got there?" Eddie pointed at our boxes.

"Just office supplies," Nate said.

The guys leaned forward to see for a look-see.

"Where'd you find all that?"

"In the dumpsters."

Eddie laughed. "In the basura? Yeah, right." He
hawked a loogie on the ground. "I think you güeros
stole that shit."

"We didn't steal it," Nate swore. "It was in the
dumpsters.

"What's your problem?" I demanded. I'd had enough of
Nate's laid-back approach. These were just a bunch of
kids our age acting like they were full-on cholos.
"It's our stuff, so what the fuck?"

Eddie stepped closer. "I ain't got no problem, homes.
But check it out... Either give up that shit or we're
calling la hura."

"Call the cops," I said, challenging his bluff. "We
ain't done nothing. I turned to leave. "C'mon, let's
split."

"Hold up, vato!" Eddie put up his arm like he had
super powers. "You ain't going nowhere."

"Hey, look, we don't want any trouble," Nate said.
"Let's be cool."

"Orale! We're trying to be cool." Eddie grabbed the
Nerf ball from Javie. "Tell you guys what... We play
you a game of touch and the winner gets the shit."
He tossed the football up and caught it, flashing an
menacing grin while the other two laughed. "You
güeros know how to play football, don't ya?"

"What the fuck?" I was indignant. "This is bullshit. We found the stuff. It's ours."

"You found it, you ripped it off..." Eddie shrugged.
"Who knows? Who gives a fuck. But you ain't getting
it outa here unless you beat us fair and square." He
hawked another loogie.

Nate and I enxchanged glances. It was a set-up and
we knew it.

"That's cool and all," Nate said. "But we're outnumbered." He pointed at Joey. "He's only eight."

As soon as Joey realized we were talking about him,

he piped up. "I can play!"

Nate and I glared at him.

"No, you're too little." Then to Eddie, "He's too little."

"The kid says he can play, so let him play," Javie said. "Don't be panocha."

"Let him cover the quarterback, if you think he can't hang," added Oscar.

I looked at Nate. Nate looked at me. We looked at Joey. Joey looked at us. We looked at the other guys. They were smiling. We were not. Even though it was a trap, we had no choice but to play their game.

"Okay, let's get it over with."

In the field, Eddie set the ball down to form a line of scrimmage. We lined up next to the ball. And that's when the fun began.

"Look at these goofy ass güeros," Javie said. "Check out their clodhoppers!"

Hahahahahaha.

The pregame entertainment was capping on the white-boys. We were so used to this shit that it didn't even faze us anymore.

To prove what a bunch of dweebs we were, Oscar hopped around in a circle chanting, "Da dum da dum da dum da dum," over and over. You know, cause that was how we walked.

Hahahahahahaha.

"Hey, don't make fun of the güeros." Javie was suddenly serious. "It's not their fault they're so poor. I saw their mother kicking a can down the street the other day and I asked her what she was doing and she said, Moving."

Hahahaha.

"And their father was chasing after trying to get the can for the two cent deposit!"

Hahaha.

"So he can buy a biscuit for dinner!"

Hahahahahaha.

They were really enjoying themselves. But just when it seemed like the game would never start, they finally lined up for the hike. Eddie was quarterback. He licked his fingers and rubbed his hands together like he was Terry Bradshaw.

"Red dog, forty two!" he shouted. "Red dog, forty two! Hut one, hut two, hut, hut, hut... HIKE!"

Javier and Oscar charged into the field. Nate was tight on Javie. I was laying back. I didn't see much point. Eddie threw the ball to Oscar, but he was too uncoordinated and the ball hit the ground.

"Incomplete!"

On second down, Eddie threw to Javie, but Nate deflected the pass.

"Third down!"

As we lined up for the next snap, I was surprised. I thought these guys would play better, seeing as how they were so gung-ho about the game. I was struck by the notion that we might actually have a chance at winning and keeping our stuff.

I decided the next play was going to another no-gainer.

Eddie and his teammates went into a huddle and came out giggling. At the snap, Oscar ran wide. This time I was a shadow on his back. It wasn't hard to keep up with him, though. He was sweating like crazy and I could hear his heavy breathing. I looked over my shoulder to see what Eddie was doing. Like a real trooper, Joey was jumping up and down in front of him. Nate was keeping a good watch on Javie. Out of the corner of my eye, I saw Oscar cut right towards me. I tried to move out of his way, but he shoulder-blocked me. Hard.

I hit the grass.

Unprotected, Oscar caught the ball and waddled down the field until he'd gone far enough to call a touch-down.

"Motherfucker!"

I pushed myself off the ground.

"What the fuck? I thought we were playing touch? Cheating motherfuckers!"

As I shouted more profanities, everybody ran towards me. Eddie got right in my face.

"Who you calling cheaters, pinche güero?" His breath smelled like the back of a Chinese restaurant.

"What the fuck?" I didn't know what else to say. I was pissed, but Eddie was bigger than me. I tried to remember all the fights I'd seen in real-life, to figure what to do. They always started off with the face-off. Most of the time, they never came to blows. It was all about mad-dogging each other and talking shit. And then an adult would break it up. But we were the only ones around. There were no adults to intervene.

"He cheated," I managed to get out. I had to say something.

"That's how the game's played, homes," Javie said with indignation. "It's not our fault you don't know the rules."

Oscar snickered. "Yeah, man. You fell. Everybody saw it."

In the middle of the circle it was hot. I was sweating in my ears. More than anything I just wanted to go home and drink a glass of ice-cold Kool-Aid in front of the TV.

"C'mon, dudes. He didn't mean to start shit." Nate grabbed my arm. "We forfeit."

"If you forfeit, we win," Oscar pointed out.

I thought about what I had in my box and didn't care anymore. "Fuck this." I started walking.

Eddie lifted his arms in the air. "Pinche panocha!"

Oscar and Javie joined him in a victory cheer, breathing heavy into their cupped hands to recreate the roar of an audience.

"We win!"

"Yeah, the gold medal for cheating," I mumbled out of earshot.

Nate grabbed Joey by the back of his shirt and we bolted for the fence. On the sidewalk, we watched them pick through the boxes. But they didn't seem too happy with their winnings. They tossed the contents into the street.

"Oh, man," Nate said. "Those were good colored pencils."

"Fucking wetbacks!" I yelled. "Fuck you and your whore mothers!"

We took off running.

16

3.

Two days later, we were coming home from another free meal at McDonald's, thanks to the US dominance in gymnastics. We'd started going to a different McDonald's, on the other side of the freeway. More than twenty blocks away. It was a major hike, but we didn't want to risk running into Eddie again.

As soon as we walked through the front door, Mom lined us up along the kitchen counter, execution style. She looked us each in the eye, one at a time, as she read the charges.

"Two detectives from the Temple City police department stopped by today. Asking about som vandalism at Emerson school."

We tried to look as innocent as possible and kept our mouths shut.

"Said some kids broke into a supply room, vandalized it and threw office supplies into the street."

We took turns staring at the ceiling, at the wall, at the floor... anywhere but straight ahead.

"You know anything about that?"

She looked me dead in the eye.

I shook my head furiously. Nate glared at me. It was well-established that I was the one to crack under pressure.

"Well, they have witnesses," Mom continued. "These kids said they saw the whole thing." She paused.

I bit my tongue and shuffled in place.

"They said it was three boys with blonde hair."

It was getting harder to contain the confession that was rising to the surface.

"So?"

"So..." Mom opened the cupboard. "Well, let's see..." She set four boxes of pens on the table, the ones we'd hidden underneath our bunkbed. "If you all didn't have anything to do with it, how do you explain these?"

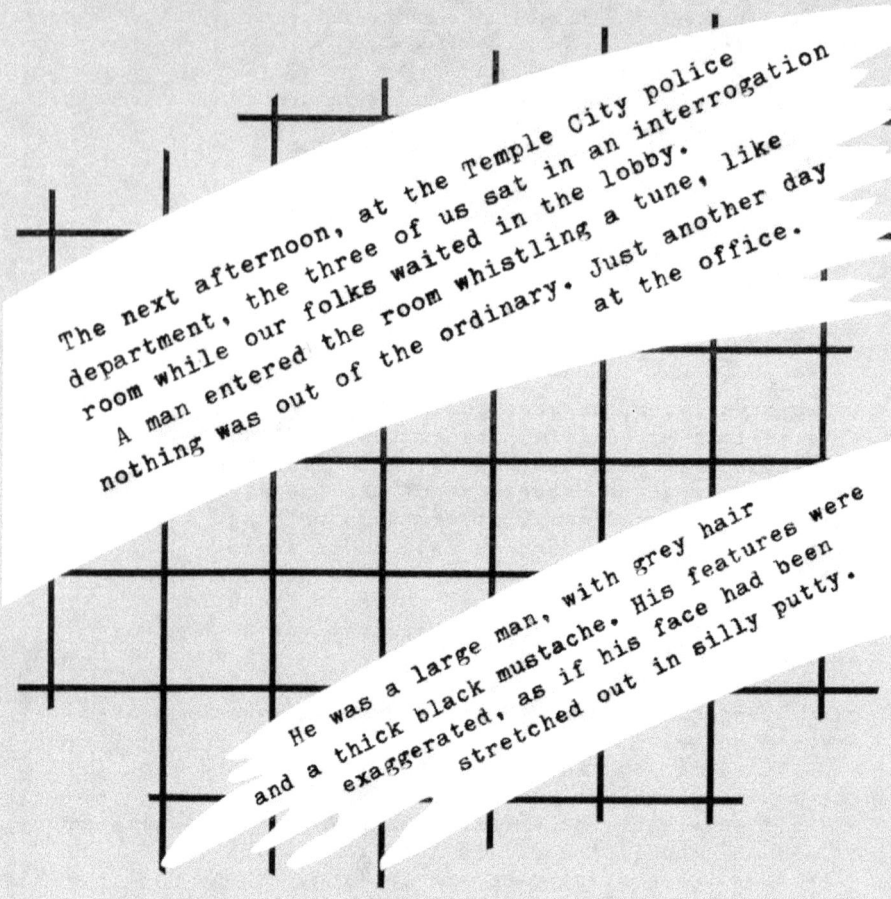

The next afternoon, at the Temple City police department, the three of us sat in an interrogation room while our folks waited in the lobby. A man entered the room whistling a tune, like nothing was out of the ordinary. Just another day at the office.

He was a large man, with grey hair and a thick black mustache. His features were exaggerated, as if his face had been stretched out in silly putty.

In one hand he clutched a cup of coffee.
In the other, a manila folder that he held like a raunchy piece of fish. As he casually sat down on the edge of the table, he dangled his right leg over the side. Sipped his coffee. Straightened the crease in his slacks.
"So," he finally said. "Why'd you boys do it?"
Nate glared at me. The plan was to keep our mouths shut. But when the detective looked me in the eyes, I had to say something.
"Just bored."
"Well, you'll be a lot more bored in jail." His tone went from friendly old guy to something more severe. "Cause that's where you three are headed. You may think you're too young to face the consequences of your actions, but you can't just run around like a pack of wild dogs and get away with vandalism and

theft and..." He opened the folder. "It says here
you were caught shoplifting a few months back. And
setting fires?" He looked up from the paperwork.
"Breaking and entering?" He cleared his throat.
"Listen, I know what it's like. I was young once.
Boys will be boys. But I'm here to tell you, I see
the path you boys are on--I see it every day. No
matter what you think, it's not going to lead you
anywhere you want to be. You're not smart enough to
fight the law. You can't win at this game. Trust me.
You know what it's like in jail?"

"I've seen moves," I said, since I thought he was
still talking to me.

"Movies!" The detective guffawed. "Son, you can't
believe everything you see in the movies. In fact,
I think you boys need a taste of the real thing."
The detective drained his mug and stood up. "Follow
me."

He directed us into another office where we were
fingerprinted and had our pictures taken.

"This is what it's like to get booked," he said.
"Now your names are in the system, so the next time
you do something wrong, you'll already have one strike
against you."

After they'd taken all our information down, the
detective led us into a larger room.

"This is where we house the prisoners."

We walked past a cell in the center of the room
occupied by a burly Mexican who sat hunched over,
grumbling to himself. A mound of hairy flesh wrapped
in a dingy white tank top. When the man saw us go
past his cell, he lifted his head and smiled.

"This is it, boys." The detective stuck a key into
the lock of a large windowless door. It swung open
with a prolonged squeal. "Let's see how bored you
get in here."

Heads down, we filed into the small concrete room.
The door sqeauled again as it slammed shut.

Joey crouched in the corner. I paced the floor
nervously, scanning the white walls, as if I could
find a way to escape. I tried to play it cool, but
I was scared.

"I'm bored," I said and laughed nervously.

"Shut it, asswipe," Nate told me.

I sat down.

"You think they'll take us to McDonald's afterwards?"
asked Joey.

"Stupid." I didn't even want to think what was going
to happen to our collection of game cards.

Joey pulled a roll of candy from his pocket. "Look
what I got." He held up one of the packets of Sweet

Tarts he'd bought at the corner store with his cut of the marker money.

"Lemme have some," I said. "The white ones."

Joey tapped a third of the roll into each of our palms and we sat there sucking on the tarts, letting them dissolve slowly on our tongues to maximize the sugar intake while we served our time.

EMMAUS SUCKED HARDCORE.

Since we were getting picked on so much in the public school, our folks finagled a way to send us to a school in Alhambra, where the upper-class white people lived. But things weren't much better at Emmaus Lutheran. The kids there knew we didn't belong. We had the stink of poverty and ridicule on us. And they had their own methods for keeping the weaker kids down: sarcasm.

Even though I laughed along, because I wanted to be friends, I knew there was something deeper in their cracks that stung worse than outright insults.

The Emmaus kids congratulated Nate and me for bringing our lunches in discarded bread bags and wrinkled paper sacks instead of fancy lunchboxes with cartoon characters emblazoned in the metal. While they wore Levi's and OP shirts, Nate and I sported highwater Toughskins with holes in the knees. Every day, the cool kids--Patrick, John, Jeremy and Scott--told us how styling our threads were. At first, we had little boy haircuts, parted at the side and slicked down--mine with the inevitable cowlick. But our new classmates had longer hair, asymmetrical bowlcuts. And they wore Vans. Chukkas were for little kids who were still dressed by their parents. Those were the kinds of shoes we wore.

I tried to fit in at the new school. I grew my hair out and pleaded with my folks to buy me cooler clothes and a real lunchbox, plus those cool Trapper Keepers with album covers on the front.

I started listening to metal. Patrick's older brother was already hanging out in Hollywood and report-
ing back on the new bands coming out, as well as the
ones from England.

But nothing impressed the guys at Emmaus.

I once brought my baseball card collection to school
for show and tell. I had over a thousand cards, but
Patrick and Scott said they were worthless because
instead of keeping them in pristine condition and
storing the valuable players in plastic sleeves, I
scattered my cards on the floor of my room and slid
into the pile like I was stealing second. This activ-
ity, while loads of fun, frayed the edges and creased
the corners, rendering them useless in their eyes.

One day I went to school with my new Iron Maiden
shirt under my uniform. For months, I'd been begging
Mom to buy me the shirt that had been hanging on the
wall of Music Plus. I was so proud when I finally got
it. But when the guys at school saw it, Patrick
asked me, "Why are you wearing a Maiden shirt?"

They were my favorite group. I had all their albums,
even several import EPs.

"So?"

I didn't understand.

"You may listen to Maiden, but you're too lame to
get Maiden."

Later that afternoon, while listening to The Number
of the Beast for the hundredth time, I wondered what
I was missing.

Our classmates at Emmaus weren't allowed to hang
out with us after school. The few times they did, we
took them panhandling or set things on fire. One kid
fell off the freeway wall and impaled his leg on the
chainlink fence. His father threatened to sue, but
let it go when he realized we had nothing to take.

We were pariahs.

White trash.

So in the afternoons, we were back on the street,
where the neighborhood kids made us pay a hefty toll
to ride our bikes and play games in their turf.

During the day, while the old man was at work and
Mom was out selling Avon, our house became the local
hangout. Unsupervised, we had free reign of the place.
All the kids from the neighborhood congregated in our
living room to watch movies and raise hell, if the
opportunity arose.

A TOTALLY DIFFERENT HEAD

"HEY, I'M GONNA USE YOUR PHONE," Oscar said. He was sitting on the couch next to Javier. Brewster's Millions was in the VCR.

I watched from the rocking chair. "I'm not supposed to let you guys use the phone anymore," I told him without taking my eyes off the screen. We all had our own theories on how to blow thirty million dollars in thirty days. Mine was foolproof: Start a band and hire the most infamous rockers for the members. We'd stage benefit concerts around the world that would rival anything by KISS. I'd blow the rest living a rock and roll lifestyle like Mötley Crüe. It seemed so simple that I couldn't understand why it took Monty so long to unload his loot.

"Let him use the phone, homes," Javier chimed in. "Fuck what your mom says."

"Sorry, Charlie."

Oscar liked to call 976 numbers. A few months back, he was on the phone every day for hours at a stretch. And then the bill showed up. Mom freaked out so bad she ran through the house waving the bill in the air like it was on fire, screaming, "Five hundred dollars! Five! Hundred! Dollars!" Practically ripped the phones out of the wall.

"Yeah, let me use the phone," Oscar persisted. "I gotta call this chick I met in Montebello."

"Yeah, right."

"C'mon. I'll let you have some of my soda." Oscar waved a can of Sunkist tantalizingly.

"I hate orange soda."

"Don't be a pendajo," Javier said. "Let him use the phone."

"Hmmm, let me think about it." I pretended to contemplate the smoke stains on the ceiling. "Uhhh... no!"

"Fuck you, guero." Oscar spit a stream of soda onto the carpet.

"That's it!" I leapt out of the chair and opened the front door, let it swing wide. "Get the fuck out. I'm sick of you guys disrespecting my house."

Javier laughed. "You fuck shit up more than anybody."

"Yeah, well I live here and you don't."

"Whatever. We're here to see NayGyver anyway. Not your panocha ass."

"Nate's outside." I gestured out the door. "Why don't you dicks join him."

They took their sweet time about it. I slammed the door after them and went back to the movie. I calculated how much I could waste buying really expensive guitars and smashing them on stage like Paul Stanley.

When the movie was over I watched an episode of Bonanza. The phone rang. I ignored the first four peels as Pa Cartwright readied the team for a trip to Virginia City, leaving Hoss and Little Joe in charge of the ranch. Hilarious mishaps were sure to follow and I didn't feel like answering the phone anyway. It was probably just one of Mom's Avon customers. But right at the sixth ring, the show went to commercial, so I picked up.

"Go."

"Can I please speak with Claudia?" a girl's soft voice asked.

It was the politeness that made me suspicious.

"And who might this be?" I responded in a mockingly dignified tone.

"It's me," the voice replied.

"Oh yeah? Me who?" I knew I was getting taken for a ride but decided to play along, at least during the commercials.

"Me." The voice was firmer this time. Insistent.

"Is this Lupe?" I asked, getting bored. Lupe was

23

Claudia's friend from across the street. She was a
real pain in the ass. "Stop fucking around, Lupe."

"This isn't Lupe. It's me."

"You already said that." I was losing interest.
Sometimes a crank call was good for a few laughs, but
this one had little potential. "You can't come up
with anything better than that?" I made a few farting
noises.

"No really. It's me!"

"I'm gonna hang up if you don't say something else
in 5... 4..."

"You don't understand." She was getting frantic.
"That's my name. I'm a friend of Claudia. From--"

I'd had enough. "Fuck you." I hung up as the show
came back on.

A few hours later, during a rerun of Happy Days,
my sister came home.

"Has anybody called for me?"

"Just Lupe. She kept saying, 'This is me. This is me.'
So I hung up on her. Stupid bitch."

"Me?" Claudia tilted her head slightly. "Did she
say 'Ni'?"

"That's what I said."

"No, not 'me'. 'Ni'?"

"What the fuck are you talking about?"

"'Ni'! I made a friend at school today. Her name is
'Ni'. She said she was going to call me."

"You mean like--" I pointed at my knee.

"Yeah! N-I Ni!"

"What kind of fucking name is that?"

"She's Chinese."

"Oh."

"I can't believe you hung up on her!" A torrent of
tears instantly erupted from behind the mop of curls
covering her face. "Now she's never going to call me
again!"

"Wow. Gee... Sorry." I tried not to laugh as Claudia
ran to her room. "If you don't want me to hang up on
your friends, tell them to get names that make sense!"
I called after her.

Whatever.

I went back to the TV. Richie was pleading with the
Fonz to help him and Potsie out of another jam they'd
gotten in with Ralph the Mouth. Meanwhile, Chachi was
acting slick to get up Joanie's skirt.

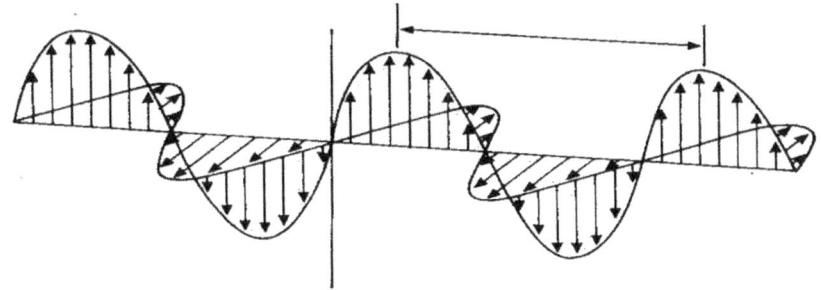

During a commercial, I fixed a bowl of hot-buttered
Cheerios. My speciality. When the show was over, I
went for an after snack smoke. I got one of the Kools
I'd swiped from the old man's pack. But I was out of
matches. So I hit the gas on the stove and leaned
down to the flame.

It happened so fast I barely heard the sizzle before
I smelled that distinctive odor of burnt hair.

At first, I was afraid to even look in the mirror. I
had to sneak up on my reflection.

I knew it was going to be bad, but I was shocked by
what I'd done to myself. In one instant act of stu-
pidity, I looked like a balding man still trying to
live the dream. My bangs were gone and the front of
my head was singed to the crown.

As I ran my hand over the stubble, I winced and took
a drag from the cigarette, not even enjoying it, what
with all the trouble it had caused me.

Oh, what a price to pay for such a simple lesson
learned!

I'd just spent an entire year letting my hair grow
out from the Kevin Bacon phase I went through in 8th
grade, and now, I was further back than when I started.

But the worst part, the aspect of my misfortune
that hit the hardest, was that I was starting high
school in less than a month. That meant so long to my
hope of fitting in with the other metalheads. How
was anybody supposed to know what a rocker I was if I
was sporting a buzz cut?

I thought of Rob Halford, but it was little conso-
lation. I wanted to look like Eddie Van Halen or
Vince Neil.

Oh man, I was bummed.

I flicked the cigarette into the sink just as Oscar
and Javier returned.

"Hey, what stinks?" Oscar shouted.

"Oh, look at your head!" Javier chortled.

Then Oscar joined in.

When they saw what I'd done to my hair, they could-
n't stop laughing.

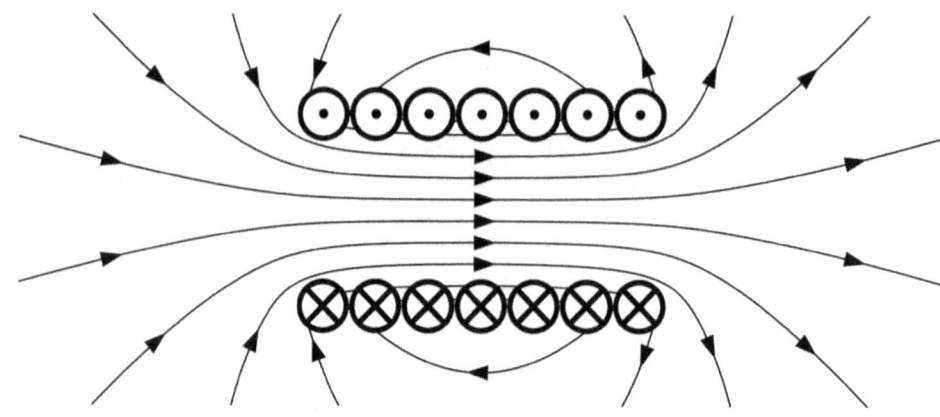

"That's fucked up!"

"You look like... like..." Javier couldn't even come up with a decent cap he was bent over laughing so hard.

They laughed for ten minutes straight.

When they finally settled down, Oscar slapped me on the back and said assuredly, "Don't worry, homes. I can fix it."

"How can you possibly fix this?" I asked solemnly.

"I know how to style hair."

"Really? Nah, bullshit."

"There's plenty you don't know about me."

"Yeah, it's true," Javier swore.

Oscar went on to present a convincing rundown of his expertise, claiming that his sister was a hair-dresser, which I knew was true, and that she had taught him how to cut and style hair.

Javier claimed that Oscar even sculpted his own budding pompadour.

Figuring there wasn't much I had to lose, I agreed to let him have a whack at it.

I sat on a kitchen chair while they walked around me, pointing at my head and contemplating the various hairdos that could be created out of what was left.

"Maybe something new wave?" Javier suggested.

"That would be fresh," echoed Oscar.

"You could even make a tail out of what's left on the back of your head."

"A tail?" I thought of Johnny Slash from Square Pegs.

"I can totally pull off that look," Oscar said.

"Totally."

I was still dubious, but... "Ah, fuck it. Do it."

Javier found a pair of children's saftey scissors, which didn't have much of an edge, but all we could find. In the process, Oscar pulled out as much as he cut.

"Hey! That shit fucking hurts!" I yelled with each yank.

"You want it to look good, yeah?" Oscar choked back
a snicker as he went through the motions of a hair-
dresser: here a snip, there a snip... a yank here, a
yank there...

"Ow, fucker!"

"Hijole!"

When he was finished, I went to the bathroom to
check out my new look. I saw my reflection and ran
through the house, looking for the culprits.

"Motherfuckers! What'd you do to my head!"

I charged out the back door. Oscar and Javier were
halfway down the driveway.

"Look at your head!" Oscar yelled as the gate crashed
metal on metal. Javier was laughing so hard he could
barely stay on his feet.

"Fuckers! Motherfucking mother FUCKERS!"

When the old man got home that evening, he examined
the butcher job.

"You look like a cancer patient. Why'd you let them
do this to you?"

I shrugged. "It was fucked up already."

"What's this back here?"

"A tail."

The old man looked at me over his glasses. "What
are you, a jackass?"

With Mom's sewing scissors, he tried to straighten
the uneven strands on the side and remove the tufts
that protruded from my scalp like crab grass.

But it was no use.

The next day I went to the barbershop where we used
to get our little boy haircuts. The barber stifled a
chuckle and pulled out the clippers.

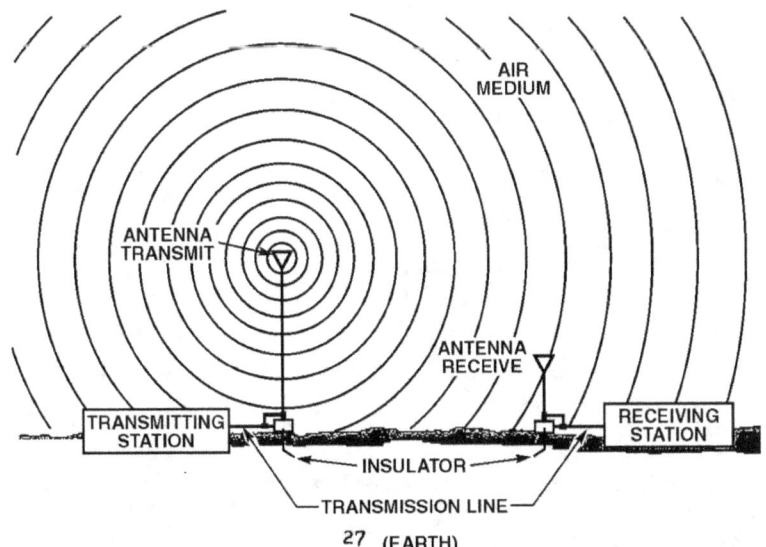

27 (EARTH)

WE WERE ALWAYS RUNNING AWAY FROM RICK. Through yards
and over fences, on rooftops and under cars... we hid
in bushes and behind dumpsters. The streets were our
playing field. Up Columbia to the freeway ramp, down
Hellman and across Jackson--anywhere was a hiding
place. There were no safety zones and the only way to
win was to make it back to the house without getting
caught. Even though we did our best, it wasn't easy
to beat Rick. Nimble and adroit, he was an excellent
hunter. And he was so gung-ho about the game that he
was always It. You never knew where he'd pop up or out
of in his pursuit. He could be lurking in the shadows
or behind any corner, ready to strike when you least
expected it. Nate and I usually made it home, but
Joey was a regular prisoner. The POW. We tried sometimes to help him escape, but when it came to Ditch Em,
it was every man for himself.

Ditch Em was Rick's invention. His version of War.

Growing up, Rick was a constant fixture at our house.
since his family moved in two doors down. In those
days, I was the neighborhood welcoming committee.
Shortly after they arrived, I hid behind Mrs Garcia's
fence and threw eggs at Rick and his brothers when
they were hanging out in their back yard. Nate was on
the front porch when Rick walked up to our gate.

"Is that your brother hiding behind the tree?"

"Sort of. We're more like cousins."

"Well, he's a real asshole."

"I know. I hate him too."

Because he was older, four years my senior, Rick
quickly presented himself as a guardian for my brothers
and me. When we ran the streets after school, Rick
promised Mom to make sure we didn't get into trouble.

"Don't worry, Mrs Jan," he used to tell her earnestly
each time we walked out the front gate. "I'll look
after the rugrats."

As far as she could tell, Rick was a good influence.
Around adults he was careful to mind his manners. But
once we were out of sight, Rick was a ceaseless pro-
vocateur. A Peter Pan to our Lost Boys.

Rick initiated some of the best capers.

When we weren't embroiled in an epic game of Ditch
Em, we rode our BMX bikes to one of the many local
schools and climbed the roofs. In the empty dirt lots
around town, we carved out off-road courses and practiced jumps and wheelies and other tricks. Rick had
the coolest bike on the street. A Mongoose, with red
pads on the handlebars and the cross bar and an alloy
frame that had pegs on the axles so he could do stunts
or carry a passenger.

Rick showed us how to scale the fence that barri-
caded the Wash and we rode our bikes through the
series of concrete channels that drained the entire
San Gabriel Valley and flowed into Whittier Narrows,
a swampy, bug-infested recreation area that the locals
called Marrano Beach--Filthy Pig Beach. In the scummy
water, we'd play Rambo. But there were never enough
BB guns to go around, so one of us had to be the prey
while the others took pot shots along the gravel edge.

For a while there, Rick was our best friend. But
the summer before his last year in high school, Rick
was riding his Mongoose across New Avenue and got
broadsided by an RTD bus. Never even saw it coming.
Projected almost thirty feet, he survived, miracul-
ously, with multiple broken limbs and lacerations
over his face and torso that required hundreds of
stitches. He was in the hospital for a month. The
doctors said he was lucky to be alive. The bus hit
him so hard, the frame of his bike was bent in half.

After the accident, Rick was never the same. When
he got home from the hospital, there were no more games
of hide and seek. No more Ditch Em. No more bike rides
and no more playing in the wilderness of Garvey Ranch
Park. He began acting like a military man and talked
about joining the Army as soon as he graduated. The
old man brought him several pairs of regulation uni-
forms and combat boots. Rick wore them every day. At

San Gabriel High that year, he was known as Major Tom.
He read Soldier of Fortune magazine and claimed that
once he got through Basic Training, he was going to
join the Green Berets.

Rick's folks replaced his mangled bike with a moped
and he started driving out to the reserve center in
El Monte to visit the old man at work each day after
school. He had gone there in the past, with us during
summer vacation, when the reservists brought their
kids to work. But once he planned to sign up, Rick
perceived his time as the center as a prerequisite
to his future career.

And we weren't invited.

The only times we were allowed to tag along was if
we played one of his new games, which were more so-
phisticated, but no less duplicitous.

"WANNA GO FOR A JOYRIDE?"

Rick and I were lounging on a stack of decommiss-
ioned C-rations, ripping open the containers with a
buck knife and tossing aside the cans of mysterious
meat to get at the cookies and crackers. When Rick
suggested we take one of the Army Jeeps out for a
spin, I leapt to my feet.

"Hell yeah!"

Since Rick first told us that he'd figured out how
to hotwire the Jeeps, I'd been waiting for an opportunity to be a part of the action. It seemed like Rick
was always bragging about the cool things he was doing
at the reserve center where my dad worked. But he
rarely let my brothers or me tag along. So this was
my chance and I was ready to go.

"You hafta do something for me in return." Rick had
a sinister laugh that sent shivers.

I kicked a can of salisbury steak across the asphalt.
"What's it gonna be this time?"

"I'll explain later. Let's go."

We walked to the motor pool, where the fleet of cam-
ouflaged pick-ups, tractor trailers, cargo trucks and
personnel carriers were lined up. Along the outside
was an armada of Jeeps.

Except for the two week training session in the
summer, when all the weekend warriors convoyed out
to the desert to play soldier, the vehicles lay dor-
mant. The steering wheels were chained and padlocked
to the gear shifters. The keys for the locks were
secured in the major's office. Not even my father,
a sergeant first class, had access to them.

But Rick figured out a way around this security
measure.

"Some of the chains are slack enough that you can
still turn the steering wheel," Rick explained as we
walked around the Jeeps. "So you can't make sharp
turns, and you can't get past third gear, but you
can still drive around."

I understood very little of what he was saying. As
long as I got to drive a Jeep, I didn't care about the
specifics.

We picked out a Jeep with the loosest chain. Side
by side, we sat in the driver's seat. Rick was going
to help me drive. Even though I'd never driven a car
before, I assured him that I'd picked up enough of the
basics from the back seat. But Rick said it was part
of the deal.

"An Army Jeep has a manual transmission and no pow-
er steering."

Since I knew nothing about clutches or shifting gears
the plan was for Rick to handle the gears while I
pushed in the clutch.

After he'd gone through the process step by step,
Rick said, "But here's the deal... I'll shift the
gears so you can drive, but afterwards, you're gonna
shift my gears."

"Huh?"

"Don't be stupid. I'm gonna work your stick..." He
pointed at the gear shifter. "Then, you're gonna work
my stick." He pointed at his crotch and smiled. "A
joyride for a joyride. You know the drill."

Unfortunately, I did. But I really wanted to drive
a Jeep. I thought about it for a minute and decided,
what the hell. I'd done more for less. I was ready
to cruise.

Rick started up the engine, which sputtered and
rumbled into life.

"Let's go!" I shouted and revved the engine.

I was expecting to take off like a rocket, but
the Jeep progressed slowly, the gears grinding as I
struggled to coordinate the clutch with Rick's shifting. We cruised along the fence that encircled the

reserve center, a dust cloud in our wake. On the first turn, the back of the Jeep fishtailed around the curve and a cascade of gravel pinged the chainlink.

"Even it out!" Rick told me.

We approached a long straightaway and I put the pedal to the medal. The transmission whined in revolt, but I managed to get up to 35 mph.

"Yeah!" I hollered into the wind. "We're rolling now!"

As we approached the next turn, Rick said, "Get ready to start pulling hard on the wheel. Push the clutch in and remember to release slowly."

The multiple requests left me flummoxed. I was only interested in speed. The rest of this driving stuff was all blahblahblah.

Still, I tried to work the clutch and turn at the same time. But I wasn't able to do both tasks quick enough. I felt the vehicle moving beneath me against my will. Rick was screaming at me.

"Turn the wheel! Hit the brakes! Turn! Turn hard!"

It was clear in that flash of time I was out of my depth. Rick tried to commandeer the wheel.

"Take your foot off the gas!"

"Oh."

I hit the brakes instead. The Jeep went into a tail spin. Rick turned the wheel in the opposite direction. We were heading towards a row of personnel carriers.

"Take you foot off the brake!"

"What?"

It was too late.

We braced for impact.

For several minutes, or maybe it was just seconds, we sat there in a cloud of dust. We weren't moving anymore, but I still felt a wave of propulsion inside my guts.

When I opened my eyes, I was gripping the steering wheel, my hands right next to Rick's.

He looked how I felt.

"Let's get the fuck outa here," Rick said.

I tried to run, but my legs had mutinied from the rest of my body. As I waddled across the field, I looked over my shoulder at the wrecked Jeep. The dust was clearing, but the engine hissed like a ripe kettle.

"What are we gonna do?" I asked.

We were back where we started, next to the pile of c-rations.

"We tell your dad."

This seemed idiotic, but all I could think to do was keep running away from the scene of the crime and hope nobody saw me. That was how I usually dealt with a situation like this.

"No, it'll be alright."

When we reported the incident to the old man, he
followed us back to the accident site. We surveyed
the damage.

"What the fuck were you guys thinking?" he seethed.
"Fucking morons!"

"It's okay, Claude."

"The fuck it is. Look what you've done."

"We just gotta come up with a good story. Like
always, right?"

"How am I supposed to explain this? You've wrecked
government property! This is a federal crime! A fed-
er-al CRIME!"

I wasn't used to seeing my father so worked up, but
the whole front end of the Jeep was smashed in and the
wheels looked like they were caving in. The carrier,
on the other hand, barely had a scratch.

"I really nailed the fucker, didn't I?"

"Louis, shut up!"

"Yeah," Rick echoed the old man. "Let the adults
figure this out."

I went back to marvelling my handiwork while they
figured out a good story.

My father rubbed his forehead. "Let's see... It's
Friday, so nobody will be back until Monday. We can
just leave everything the way it is... when they show
up in the morning, we'll keep our mouths shut and maybe they'll just assume some Mexicans broke in and hot-
wired the thing. Lost control and crashed..."

"That's perfect!" Rick enthused.

"That's the only chance we got."

"You always come of with the best excuses, Claude."

"I'm sick getting sick of bailing you out of all your
hair-brained stunts."

"We were just having fun."

"It was fun alright!" I chimed in.

"Shut up," Rick snapped. "Help get rid of the evi-
dence."

We wiped our fingerprints off the steering wheel and
the gear shifter. As we left the scene of the crime, I
wondered if I would still have to fulfill my end of the
deal. Seeing as how my joyride had ended badly, it
seemed like I should get a pass. But who was I kidding?

Rick never let a debt slide.

the summer of the stalker

A KILLER WAS ON THE LOOSE.

Nate and I had just graduated from Emmaus and were heading to high school. Public high school. Mark Keppel. We were nervous. Or at least I was. Over the years, we'd heard horror stories from our neighbors, the Salazar brothers, who said the only way to protect yourself from the violence was to carry a knife. They told us about the Tradition, where the Mexicans would fight the whiteboys. But since there weren't that many white students anymore, the few that were there got it all.

I pleaded with Mom to send me to a different school, but she never had time for my concerns. The few times I got her to listen to me, she countered with a hysterical tirade about how we all had to make sacrifices since money was so tight.

We needed a distraction. And as far as distractions went, it was hard to find something better than a serial killer.

Two people had been killed a few blocks from our house.

And then some people up the street in Monterey Park got it.

Our city was under attack.

The newspapers called him the Valley Intruder at first, but after he branched out of the San Gabriel Valley and started leaving satanic markings on the walls of the houses he broke into, usually with their own blood, they changed it to the Night Stalker.

Even though we lived in a yellow house next to the freeway, which, according to the papers, were his favorite targets, we never acted scared. All the guys in the neighborhood would sit around and talk shit. How we'd beat his ass if we saw him coming through our windows at night.

"I always got my windows open," Oscar bragged.

"Come on in, meet my little friend," Rick joked, as if his BB guns could stop a real killer.

But we all laughed.

It was hot as hell that summer. As we made out like we were just waiting for a chance to take him down, in reality we couldn't sleep well with the windows open or shut.

The cops were telling people on the news to arm themselves. We all wanted guns, rifles, knives, swords, bazookas...

Then came the sketch of what the killer looked like. We saw the papers and flipped out. He could have been our friend Fernando. We were like, "Dude, are you the Night Stalker? Why you keeping that from us?"

"Man, you better watch out or they're gonna bust your ass," Javier cracked.

"They gonna bust your ass just for looking like the Night Stalker!" added Oscar.

A few days before school started, the Night Stalker was spotted downtown. People on the streets chased him into East LA, where he was nearly beaten to death right there on the pavement. By the time the cops showed up, he was begging to be arrested.

That he'd been apprehended in East LA made us all proud. Because when it came down to it, we were all from East LA.

"Don't fuck with the Mexicans," everybody was saying, as if they'd been in the crowd themselves.

That night, everybody partied hard.

The threat was over.

But high school was right around the corner.

37

Marlboro Country

ACROSS THE STREET FROM MARK KEPPEL HIGH, between a
deadend road that led to the faculty parking lot and
the freeway overpass, there was a small patch of scrub.
A few palm trees protruded from the gravel and trampled
weeds. This was Marlboro Country, where all the cool
students went to smoke. As I scanned the crowd for my
friend Carlos, I pulled a pack of Benson & Hedges out
of my jean jacket and tried to fit in.

I was still getting used to the idea of Carlos being
my friend. He was two years older than me and for as
long as I could remember, he only paid attention to
me long enough to inflict some form of humiliation.
From my first days at Emerson, Carlos had terrorized
me with vicious name-calling, menacing threats and
constant sneak attacks. His favorite was "Have a nice
trip!" And then, as I hit the ground, that laugh...
Carlos laughed like a broken lawn mower. Huyahhuyah-
huyahhuyah. Even though he lived next door to me, I

avoided him like the plague. So, two days before school
started, when he walked up to my fence and called me
over, my first instinct was to run.

"You going to Keppel this year?" he asked.

"Yeah," I said hesitantly.

"Cool. Wait for me on Monday morning and I'll walk
with you."

All weekend, I wondered what misfortune awaited me
on my first day back in public school. Carlos was one
of the bullies who made it so difficult for me to
stay at Emerson that my folks had to take us out of
the local district and move us to Emmaus, the Lutheran
school in Alhambra where I'd been going since fourth
grade. It only made sense, now that I was going to be
a freshman at Keppel, that he would return to the way
things used to be.

On Monday morning, sporting my favorite Mötley Crüe
shirt, my trusty jean jacket and a pair of checkered
Vans with the big toe busted out, I stood on the sidewalk in front of his house, resigned to whatever prank
was about to come.

Keppel was only three blocks away, and in that short
walk, Carlos explained the inner workings of student
life at the high school.

"Don't buy tickets to the pool. They'll tell you it's
on the roof of the main building, but there ain't no
pool. And stay away from the chinks. They're all in
pussy gangs. You'll see... Hey, you know how the chinks
come up with their names right?"

I shook my head.

"They drop a bunch of change on the floor and whatever they hear, that's what they call their kids.
Ching, chang, cho, ding, ling..." He let out that
laugh. Huyahuyahhuyahhuyah.

I nodded and smiled. I knew his family hated the
Asians that had been taking over the neighborhood and
especially Monterey Park. A few years back, when the
Chinese and Vietnamese immigrants first started moving
into the area, Carlos' father asked my folks to sign a
petition to ban them from buying houses on our street.
The old man told him that we weren't interested. He
didn't mention that his sister had an adopted Korean
daughter and that Mom's brother had two adopted kids
from Taiwan. Besides, I much preferred the Asian kids
over the Mexicans. Even though I couldn't understand
most of what they said and their houses smelled awful
and you had to take your shoes off when you went to
their houses, they were friendly. They didn't call me
names. And they distracted the bullies. Suddenly, a
whiteboy wasn't the lowest form of life around. But I

kept my mouth shut. I wasn't going to defend them and
risk exposing myself to more vitriol.

"Oh, and whatever you do, watch out for Picklehead."

"Picklehead?"

"Yeah. He's this narco that thinks he's a real cop.
But he ain't shit. Most of the other narcos don't care
about anything but guns and drugs, shit like that. But
Picklehead, he gets off on busting dudes for stupid
shit."

"Why do they call him Picklehead?"

"Why you think? Cause he's a chrome dome!"

Huyahuyahhuyahhuyah.

In front of the school, a guy with long hair in a
Judas Priest shirt ran up to Carlos and smacked him in
the side of the head.

"Fucker!" Carlos chased the guy around the grass.
After he got him in a headlock and gave him a noogie,
they slapped hands. "This puto is Frankie," he told me.
"He gives out free blowjobs in the bathroom."

"That's your mother, cabron." Frankie nodded at me
and extended his hand, twisting it through mine: the
homeboy shake.

I was never good at the intricate hand maneuvers but
managed to pull it off.

"Que pasa, homes. You a freshman? Wanna buy a ticket
to the pool?"

"I already told him there ain't no pool, pendejo."

"Chupa." Frankie grabbed his crotch. "I gotta get to
class. Check you later in Marlboro Country?"

"Simon."

At the main entrance, there were tents set up for new
students to pick up their schedules. I headed towards
the one labeled A-D and thanked Carlos for showing me
the ropes.

"Fuck it," he said. "You know that grassy area by the
bridge on the other side of the school?"

"Yeah." I lied.

"Cool. That's Marlboro Country. Meet me there during
lunch."

I went through my first day of high school in a daze.
Between classes, I dropped off the books the teachers
handed out at my locker, trying to memorize the comb-
ination. Carlos had told me not to put anything valuable in my locker, that former students would sell
the numbers. People got ripped off all the time.

At the lunch bell, I headed to the Marlboro Country.

As I mingled among the new faces, I wondered if I was
pressing my luck and that I should just go home. But
I spotted Carlos and Frankie. They called me over.

"Que pasa, homes?"

They were with a third guy.

"This faggot is Mark." Carlos introduced me.

Mark was a whiteboy too. He had curly brown hair and a battlefield of pimples across his face. "What's up?"

We shook hands.

Frankie was in constant motion, dancing a jig and slapping his hands against his legs, keeping a beat. "Where's the party, eh?" he asked me.

I shrugged.

"It's up my leg," Carlos said. "You can have a ball."

"Stupid."

"Let's get the fuck outa here," Mark said.

"Ditch on the first day back to school?" Frankie asked.

Mark pulled a joint out of his jacket and waved it in the air. "I got the yesca."

Frankie shook a set of keys.

"Shotgun!" Mark shouted.

"You down?" Carlos asked me.

"Fuck yeah!"

I followed my new friends to the parking lot. Mark ran and slid across the hood of a puke green Pontiac covered in KLOS and KMET stickers. He stood at the passenger door and drummed his palms on the roof.

"Andale! Andale!"

I got in the back seat with Carlos. Mark switched on the stereo while Frankie revved the engine. Aerosmith blasted out of the speakers as Frankie careened onto the street, swerving recklessly and narrowly missing several parked cars.

"Blaze it, ese!" he shouted.

Mark lit the joint and passed it to Frankie. It made the rounds and Carlos handed it to me.

"You blaze, right?"

"For sure." I took the joint and hit it like I knew what I was doing. It was my first time. The smoke burned my throat and I coughed as I handed the joint to Mark.

"It's good shit, huh?" Mark let out a plume of smoke and punched the dashboard. "Go London, dude! Go fucking London!"

"Do it! Do it!" Carlos chanted.

Frankie pulled into the opposite lane, headed into oncoming traffic.

"Mega, dude! Mega!" Mark roared his approval.

Just before we reached the first car that was blowing its horn, Frankie swerved back into his lane.

We were all laughing as the driver glared.

On Almansor, we hit a roadblock. The street was congested with Asian teenagers.

"What the fuck is going on with the chinks?" asked Frankie.

At first it seemed as if they were just standing
around. Then they were running at each other, kicking
and punching, using kung fu, just like in a Bruce
Lee movie.

"Holy shit!" Frankie pulled over to investigate.

"The chinks have gone loco," Carlos said.

Mark crawled out the window and shouted. "Mega, dude!
Mega!"

The Asian kids let out high-pitched yelps as they
fought, elongated guttural screams that made the
action almost comical. Some of the brawlers whipped
nunchucks in the air. We saw a guy take a blow to the
head. He stumbled and fell to the pavement, blood
trickling down his face.

"Fucking A!"

"Mega!"

We watched for several more minutes until we heard
sirens.

"La hura!"

"Let's jam!"

Mark's feet were still hanging out the window as
Frankie peeled away.

For the next few hours, we cruised through the
streets of Monterey Park with the stereo blasting
until Carlos shouted, "Take me home, assholes!"

The car came to a screeching halt in front of our
houses. Carlos and I got out and stood by the driver's
side window.

"You fuckers got any fedya for gas?" Frankie asked.

Carlos pulled out the pockets of his jeans. "No,
but you can kiss the bunny."

"What about you, freshman?" Frankie asked me.

"Sorry, man."

Frankie shook his head. "Later, faggots."

I stood in the street, dazed and confused.

"So meet up tomorrow morning?" Carlos asked.

"Sure. I mean..." I hesitated to form the words to
express my grattitude.

"What, you don't wanna hang out with us?"

"No, it's not that. I just... "

Carlos reared back like he was going to punch me. I
recoiled from what I had been expecting all day.

Huyahuyahuyahhuyah...

"Don't be a faggot." Carlos socked me lightly on the
shoulder. "I'll see you in the morning."

MOM WAS IN WAY OVER HER HEAD. We were such a rotten
bunch of kids and there were too many of us. She was
outnumbered. She tried everything she could over the
years to keep us in line. She read parenting books,
developed a failed point system, went to Tough Love
seminars, even therapy. When we really got out of hand,
she threatened to take us back to the police station.
Not that we were frightened of that anymore. Nothing
worked. So she just beat the crap out of us. Used anything she could get her hands on for a weapon: belts,
hangers, forks, blunt objects or just the brute force
of her fist.

Eventually Nate and I grew taller and overshadowed
our mother. One day, she smacked Nate and he pushed
her down. She hit the floor with an OOMF! Right on her
fanny. She stopped hitting us after that. But she was
still pissed and screamed nonstop.

When she wasn't yelling at us kids, she tore into
the old man. He came home evry night to these dinner-
time gripe sessions, during which Mom eviscerated him
with her razor tongue, airing grievances from the same
inventory of frustrations: the MasterCharge debt, the
third mortgage so he could get the Cadillac he'd always
wanted, even though it was the cheapest model they had.
Then there was our behavior from the lack of his discipline, the late hours he spent at the reserve center
when she needed him at home.

"I know you hate it here. Well, guess what? I hate
it too. But this is your house as well. This is your
mess as much as it's mine!"

They'd benn through this routine so many times, we
digested these diatribes as if they were unpleasant
side dishes.

For years, this went on, Mom yelling and the old man
just sitting there taking the abuse. Until one night,
he set his fork down, calmly pushed his chair back,
lifted his plate and smashed it on the table. Pieces
of crockery and tuna casserole splattered across the
room.

"Enough!" he shouted.

While we sat paralyzed with shock at his sudden rage,
he walked out the door, got into that Cadillac Cimmaron
he loved so much, and drove away. Didn't come home that
night, or the next. Never set foot in the house again.

As much as she seemed to hate him when he was around, as soon as the old man left, Mom went crazy trying to get him back. She even tried to kill herself by swallowing a bottle of aspirins and slitting her wrist with a dull steak knife.

While she was in the hospital that night, Nate and I had a My Mom Tried to Kill Herself party.

When she came back home, all she did was cry. Right in front us, getting down on her knees and putting her head in our laps, asking us what she should do. It was embarassing and excrutiating. Nate and I would look at each other and cringe. We had no clue what she expected from us. We were the kids. They were supposed to be the adults and solve the problems.

At night, Mom would come into my room and tell me she was going to kill herself, but this time she would do it right. She went into detail, saying she would drive to the 76 and get a tank of gas, then run the garden hose from the exhaust pipe through a crack in the window. Every night for several weeks, she came into my room and talked about it. After a while, I just pretended to be asleep, hoping she'd leave me alone. Some nights, she'd tell me that the car was all gassed up and ready to go. She'd say goodbye and that she loved me and my siblings, but she just couldn't go on... I wouldn't say a word. I'd just lay there, frozen still. I'd wake up wondering if she'd actually gone through with it, not knowing if she was dead or just out delivering Avon.

Then one day, she disappeared. During the day, she was working, but at night, she'd go to these Parents Without Partners meetings, where single people with kids got together at various nightclubs around town and partied. She started bringing strange men home. We'd wake up and there'd be some random dude in the kitchen drinking coffee. "Hey there, I'm a friend of your mother."

A couple guys hung around for a while. This one guy, Eddie, he was cool. He had a lot guns. Eventually shot himself in the chest. After Eddie, there was an old bald dude who drove a Porsche. One guy lived with us for a few months. He had an extra toe on each foot. Sat around the house reading library books. One day, he stole Mom's Subaru station wagen. Just drove off and left her high and dry. A few weeks later, the police tracked him down in Texas. The car came back full of dust and gravel. And overdue library books.

the bachelor
PAD

I WAS WALKING DOWN JACKSON WHEN I SPOTTED THE OLD
man's car. It had been two months since he split the
scene and I was surprised to see him so close to the
house. Especially since he swore he'd never set foot
in the place again.
"Hey, punk!" he called to me through the open passenger window.
"What are you doing here?" I asked. "Were you at the
house?"
"Fuck no! I'm looking for you. Get in. Let's go for
a ride."
I sat down in the familiar leater seat. The luxury
of a Cadillac, even if it was only a Cimarron.
"Your mother been talking shit about me?" he asked
and turned left on Hellman.
"Yeah, she's been going ballistic."
"You believe what she's saying?" He lit a Kool with
the dash lighter and passed it to me.
"Nah." I used the last of the heat from the coil to
get a Marlboro going.
"You heard I got my own apartment, right?"
"Yeah. Mom was pissed to the gills when she found
out."
"Would you like to see it?"
"Sure. Let's go!"
At Del Mar, the old man got on the freeway and headed
east, through El Monte, over the dry river bed into La
Puente and took the Francisquito exit. We passed the
In and Out University, which I'd never seen up close
before, only the sign looming over the freeway as we
drove home from Grandma's house in Victorville.
Baldwin Park was nothing like Rosemead. The streets
were lined with apartment buildings, one after another,
two, three, even four stories high. A cinderblock wall
stretched along the sidewalk, separating the pedestr-
ians from the apartment dwellers.
I liked the look of this new territory.
The old man pulled into the driveway of a massive
blue building, one of the biggest on the block. There
was an electric gate that opened automatically from a
sensor on his windhield. He had his own designated
parking spot.

As we walked through the complex, past a swimming
pool and landscaped gardens, I was blown away. It
was hard to believe that my own father lived in a place
like this. I'd always thought of people who lived in
apartments as a different breed. Apartment people.
Not like us. Not a Baudrey. We lived in a run down
house that smelled like cat piss with rotten furniture
covered in crayon graffiti and old food stains.

The furniture in the old man's apartment was practically new. In the living room, he had a red naugahyde
bar with matching stools, a bookcase that held paper-
backs and tchotchkes, a small TV on a stand next to a
fuzzy couch and love seat. In the dining room was a
glasstop table and metal chairs.

"Where'd you get all this stuff?" I asked.

"Here and there."

He said some of it belonged to his roommate, an Army
buddy named Johnny. I looked in Johnny's room. He had
Nagel prints on the wall and his closet was full of
clothes. He was into GQ style. There were fashion magazines lying around with pages torn out and taped to
a tall mirror.

"So what do you think?" the old man asked me.

"This is awesome!"

When he asked if I wanted to spend the night, I replied, "Does the pope shit in the woods?"

"Should you let your mother know?"

"Like she'd even know I was gone."

That night, several Army buddies from the reserve
center came over. They sat around the kitchen table
drinking beer and talking shit. I'd never seen the old
man so happy, laughing with the guys, telling pussy
jokes and making cracks about their wives and kids.

I hung out in the living room with Johnny, who
showed me zippo tricks and let me practice flipping open
his balisong knife. Johnny was Filipino. He said he
knew jujitsu and could kill a man with his bare hands.

"In the Philipines, you learn martial arts at a young
age."

He showed me some of his moves. I was impressed.

"I took karate lessons at the Y once," I told him.

"Let's see your moves."

"I only went a few times."

"Maybe I can teach you some basic techniques one
day."

"That sounds cool."

"Do you smoke bud?" he asked me in church tones.

"Yeah. All the time."

Johnny pulled a small pinner out of his Marlboro
Lights box. "Let's smoke this on the way to the liquor
store."

I asked the old man for some cash.

"Goddamn kids, always hustling me for a handout." He pulled out a fiver.

I snatched the bill from his hand. "It's called child support."

"That one's a real smart ass," a guy said.

"He takes after his mother."

Johnny and I smoked the joint as we walked down Francisquito. It burned fast. But it was strong. By the time we got to Puente Avenue, I was feeling the weed. We were waiting to cross when a Mexican guy passed and sneered at Johnny, "Fucking chinks."

I could smell the beer five feet away. I looked at Johnny. The Mexican guy moved closer.

"I'm sick of you pinche chinos taking over."

I waited for the action I was sure to take place once Johnny busted out some of his jujitsu moves. This guy was in for a major shock.

But Johnny played it cool. He said nothing.

The Mexican guy leaned in real close, inches from Johnny's face. "I fucking dare you to do something." His voice was a whisper.

"I don't want no trouble," Johnny said.

I thought about the guy in Kung Fu. Johnny was going to act all meek and shit but when this guy least expected it, he was going to crack his head open.

The Mexican guy hawked a loogie on the sidewalk, just missing Johnny's shoe.

"Pinche zipper eyes," he said as he walked away.

I was flabbergasted. "Why don't you kick that guy's ass? You could've totally fucked him up. He was asking for it!"

"You can't go around beating people up just because they are having a bad day," Johnny said. "He's obviously mad about something that has nothing to do with me."

Still, I felt ripped off. What's the good of knowing how to kill a person with your bare hands if you can't prove it every chance you got?

The light changed and we crossed the street.

At Puente Liquor, where a sign promised the coldest beer in town, I picked out a package of licorice, a box of lemonheads, a Butterfinger, a Klondike bar and a bag of Doritos. Nacho cheese flavor.

"You got the munchies, huh?" Johnny asked.

"Majorly."

On the way back to the apartment, I woofed down the Klondike bar and some of the licorice. In front of the TV, I finished the chips and the candy bar. By the time I got to the licorice, my head was spinning. I was on a merry-go-round and somebody was spinning it faster and faster. If I could have used my voice I would have begged them to stop.

"How much of that shit can you eat at once?" Somebody asked me.

I tried to laugh. But the vibrations sent waves of nausea through my body. I felt spasms in my stomach, revolting against the junk food indulgence. The laughter and chatter from the men aggravated the confusion. I tried to concentrate on the TV, but the action made no sense. At one point, I stuck my head between the cushions of the couch, thinking that if my head were secure, maybe the room would stop spinning.

In a fog, I lurched to the bathroom, stumbling through the door. Over the toilet, I fell to my knees.

It came out in color-coordinated waves. Orange for the Doritos, red for the licorice, brown for the chocolate, white for the ice cream and then just yellow bile followed by a spasm of dry heaves.

And that's the last thing I remembered.

I woke up in the morning on the couch with a sheet over me. My pants were unbuttoned and my underwear was bunched up around my crotch. I went to the bathroom and straightened my clothes. Afterwards, I looked for my bag of junk food, to see if there was anything left for breakfast.

I watched the TV while the old man and Johnny drank coffee.

Later, the old man dropped me off around the corner from the house.

As I walked to the door, I noticed my seventh grade school portrait in the dirt next to the porch.

On the back were my statistics: name, age, height and hair color.

I asked my sister about it.

"Oh, Mom called the police cause she thought you ran away. I guess they dropped it or something."

I looked down at the picture, at the slicked back hair, the unavoidable cowlick, the goofy grin...

"But I don't even look like this anymore."

JUNIOR CAREERS

ADVENTURES OF A TEENAGE
DOOR-TO-DOOR CANDY SALESMAN

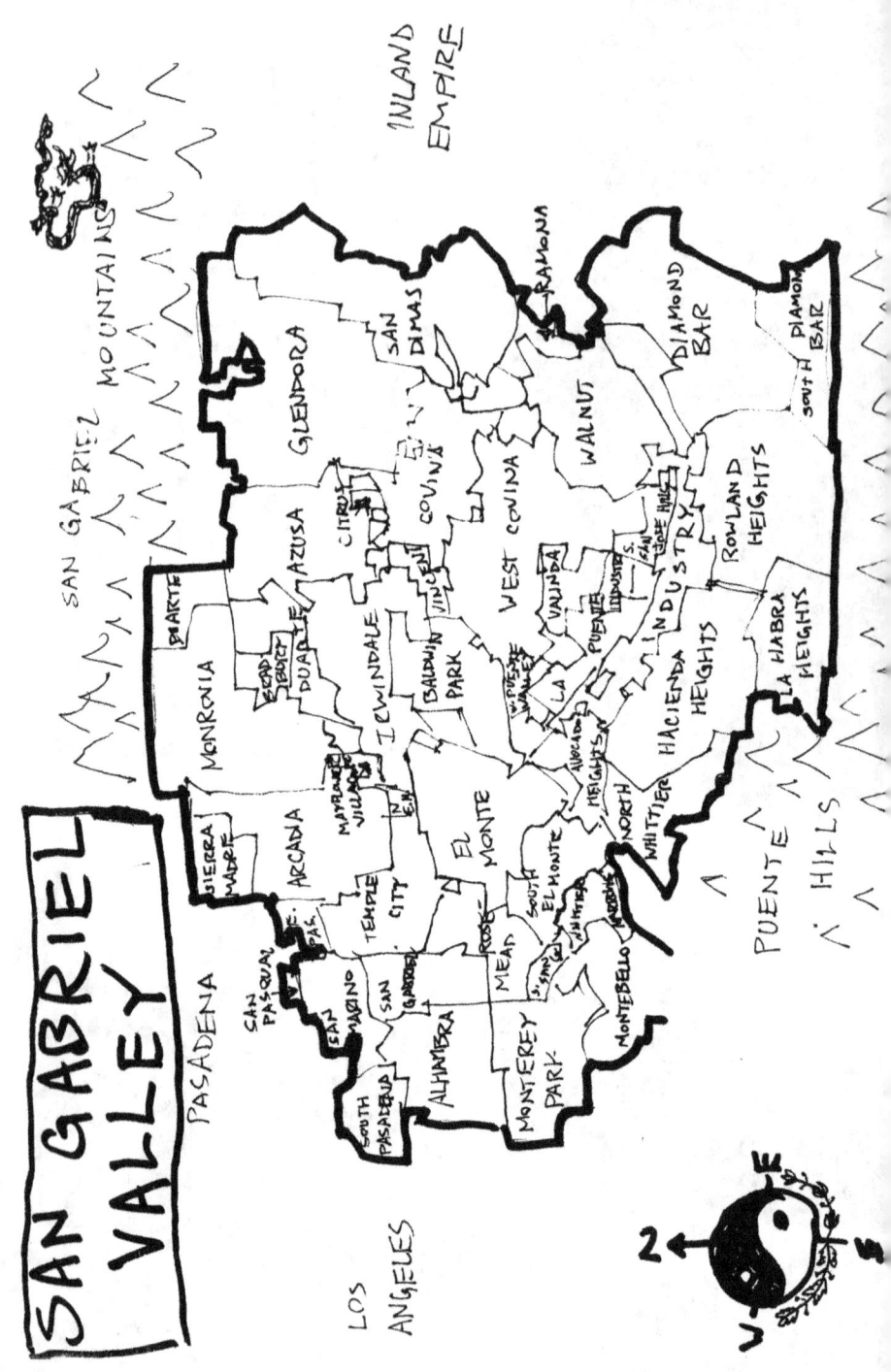

SAN GABRIEL VALLEY

INLAND EMPIRE

SAN GABRIEL MOUNTAINS

PASADENA

LOS ANGELES

SOUTH PASADENA

SAN MARINO

ALHAMBRA

MONTEREY PARK

SAN PASQUAL

SIERRA MADRE

ARCADIA

TEMPLE CITY

MONROVIA

DUARTE

BRADBURY

AZUSA

GLENDORA

SAN DIMAS

CITRUS

IRWINDALE

MAYFLOWER VILLAGE

EL MONTE

ROSEMEAD

SOUTH EL MONTE

S. SAN GABRIEL

MONTEBELLO

BALDWIN PARK

SAN VINCENT

COVINA

WEST COVINA

WALNUT

DIAMOND BAR

SOUTH DIAMOND BAR

ROWLAND HEIGHTS

LA HABRA HEIGHTS

HACIENDA HEIGHTS

INDUSTRY

LA PUENTE

W. PUENTE VALLEY

VALINDA

AVOCADO HEIGHTS

NORTH WHITTIER

S. SAN JOSE HILL

SAN JOSE HILLS

RAMONA

PUENTE HILLS

OUR TURF

Back in my early teenage years, I sold candy door to door for a company called Junior Careers.

Our turf was the San Gabriel Valley.

From the barrios of East LA, to the subdivisions of San Dimas; from the foothills of Sierra Madre, to the swamplands of Pico Rivera--every day we worked a different city.

When you'd knocked on enough doors and walked down enough streets, you could predict what your day would be like just by looking out the van window.

Every place had tells.

You might think cities like Pasadena, where the avenues are tree-lined, and not with palm trees, but the kind of trees that have billowy green leaves and trunks you can't even fit your arms around, were primo territory.

But that'd be a rookie mistake.

The best cities for candy sales were the cities with rundown apartment buildings and small crappy stucco houses that had dirt yards full of filthy, broken toys and mangy dogs--the kind of places where most of us sellers lived.

You did best when you sold to your own.

THE BOSSMAN'S RULES - No. 1

The Bossman had ten rules and "Don't waste my time" was number one on the list.

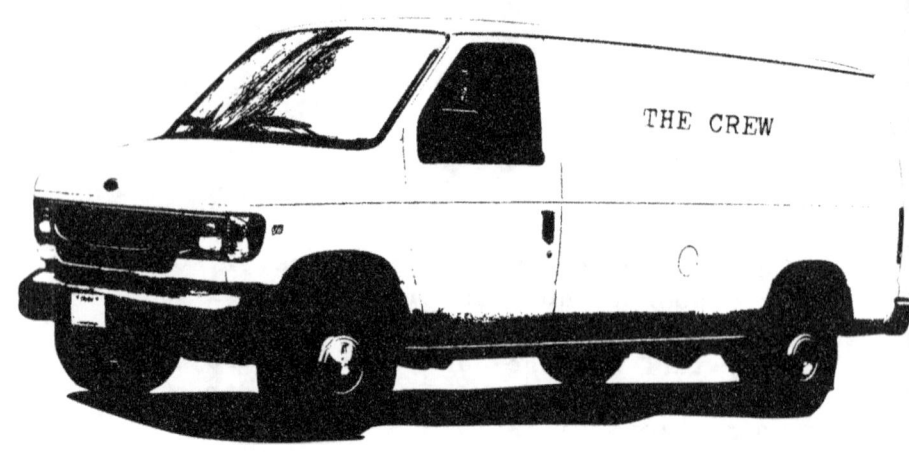

THE CREW

Every day after school, the Bossman
pulled up to the house in a beige Econoline
and blew the horn. You knew it was time to
go when you heard that unmistakable pattern:
two shorts and a long. Morse code for,
"Get the fuck out here! Right now!"

The Bossman did not like to wait.

You learned fast, if you were gonna make
it on his crew, you had to show some serious
hustle. As soon as you heard the horn blow,
you hightailed it into the back of the van
and joined the other sellers crammed against
a wall of boxes like chickens in an over-
crowded pen. If you were lucky, there'd be
a place for you on the floor, otherwise
you'd be standing, hunched over the boxes
of candy, hoping nobody pulled a lame-
brained stunt like that time Felipe yelled,
"Oh my god! Stop the van!" just as we'd
taken off. The Bossman slammed on the
brakes and we all tumbled forward into a
massive dogpile, with the boxes on top.

Everybody was freaking out.

The Bossman was shouting, "What is it?
What happened?" No doubt thinking somebody
got their fingers caught in the door again.

But then Felipe went, "Oh, a roach was
crossing the street."

We cracked up. Bigtime.

Except the Bossman.

He was pissed beyond belief.

> "If you're on the schedule and I show up
> at your house, you better be ready to work."

On any given day, there were about sixteen
of us in the van. We never made things easy
for the Bossman, dragging ass and talking
shit nonstop, as if we got paid more for
our snotty attitudes than the candy in our
boxes.

Of course, none of us really wanted to
pound the pavement for hours on end when
we could be home watching the tube or
hanging out with our friends. We did it
for the ten percent of each sale, our cut
of the profits. Slave wages, sure, but there
weren't many employment opportunities for
the under-aged.

So you dealt with it. Until you couldn't
deal with it anymore. And then you bailed.

It happened all the time...

The van pulls up to a house and a kid
comes out with a string of excuses.

"I got too much homework."

"I gotta do such and such for so and so."

"I got diarrhea."

But the only thing the Bossman hated more
than excuses was being a man short. And he
had a keen eye for bullshit. No matter what
you said, you knew it wasn't gonna be easy.
You had to be on your deathbed before he'd
even consider letting you off the hook.

Still, that didn't stop some kids from
trying their luck.

Once Mike tried to take the night off.
But instead of facing the Bossman himself,
he sent his little brother out to the van.
A cowardly act, but you could hardly
blame him, seeing as how mad the Bossman
got when you flaked on the job.

And sure enough, the Bossman went off,
shouting at the top of his lungs, in case
Mike was hiding behind the curtains.

"You tell that lazy bastard, if he
doesn't get in this van right now, I'll drag
his useless ass out here myself!"

He'd do it too! We'd seen it happen.
More than once.

He'd march right into some kid's house
and escort the culprit out by the collar
like he was a bounty hunter going after
America's Most Wanted.

This time was different though. Mike was
playing hardball. The Bossman kept yelling,
but Mike wasn't coming out.

After several minutes, the Bossman threw
his hands in the air and said, "Good riddance.
That boy was useless anyway.

Then he gave the little brother the once
over.

"What about you, kid? You want a job?
Or you gonna be useless like your brother?"

The crew was made up of mostly guys.
But there were a few girls too. Even though
they usually made more sales than us guys,
chicks never lasted as long. Everything
about the job was harder for them. From
dealing with the sleazy old dudes who
cajoled them into going inside their houses
to pitch the sale, to lugging the heavy
box, to finding a place to piss when we
were in residential areas where there were
no public restrooms. This last one was
tricky enough for a guy, though we could
just go behind a tree or in an alley.
But this wasn't an option for a girl. They
had to hold it in or ask a customer to use
their bathroom.

Because they did better, the Bossman took
it easy on the chicks. Not all the rules
applied to them. Like number three: "Dress
for success." We had to look respectable on
the job. So no rock shirts. No ripped jeans.
No cut-offs. If he didn't like how you were
dressed, the Bossman would send you back home
to change. But the girls got away with
anything. For them, the more Madonna,
the better.

THE EARNERS & THE USELESS

The Bossman had a thing against the Useless.
When I first signed up for the job, the
Bossman stopped by the house to meet with
my mom and give her the rundown, so she'd
know I'd be safe. Not that she was worried
or anything. Before I started working for
Junior Careers, I wandered the streets,
getting into trouble constantly. And then
one day I noticed a flyer stapled to a
telephone pole by Alpha Beta. According to
the bold print, Junior Careers was an
opportunity for kids twelve to sixteen to
earn extra money, win special trips, and
have fun. The prospect of a real job was
hard to pass up. So I called the number
and the next week the Bossman showed up.

He was a big guy. His brown hair was
long and wavy, like he used to be cool,
before he got old. In a loud, booming
voice, he went off about the philosophy
behind Junior Careers.

"This job is about Life Lessons. I'm
preparing you for the real world. And in
the real world, there are Earners and there
are the Useless. Those who go out and make
things happen, these are the Earners. Those
who let things happen to them, the Useless.
The Earners come home with cash in their
pockets. The Useless, they just waste their
time, and mine."

As my mom nodded her head--I could tell
she liked the sound of this spiel--the
Bossman looked me square in the eye and
asked, "So which one are you gonna be?"

"An Earner?" I asked more than said, since
I wasn't even sure what he was talking about.
But then, I woulda gone along with anything
if it meant making a few bucks.

However, after a few days, it was obvious
that I wasn't much of a salesman.

I was one of the Useless.

What money I did make went to the candy
I scarfed on the job. The same over-priced
candy I was supposed to sell.

Many a night I came home empty-handed
after blowing my meager earnings on
company goods.

It was just so hard resisting the urge to
open a box as I went along the route.
Dealing with all that candy, I got the
munchies something fierce. I'd try to
fight off the temptation, but I justified
my splurges with the fact that, since I made
ten percent of what I ate, it was kinda like
I got paid to eat candy.

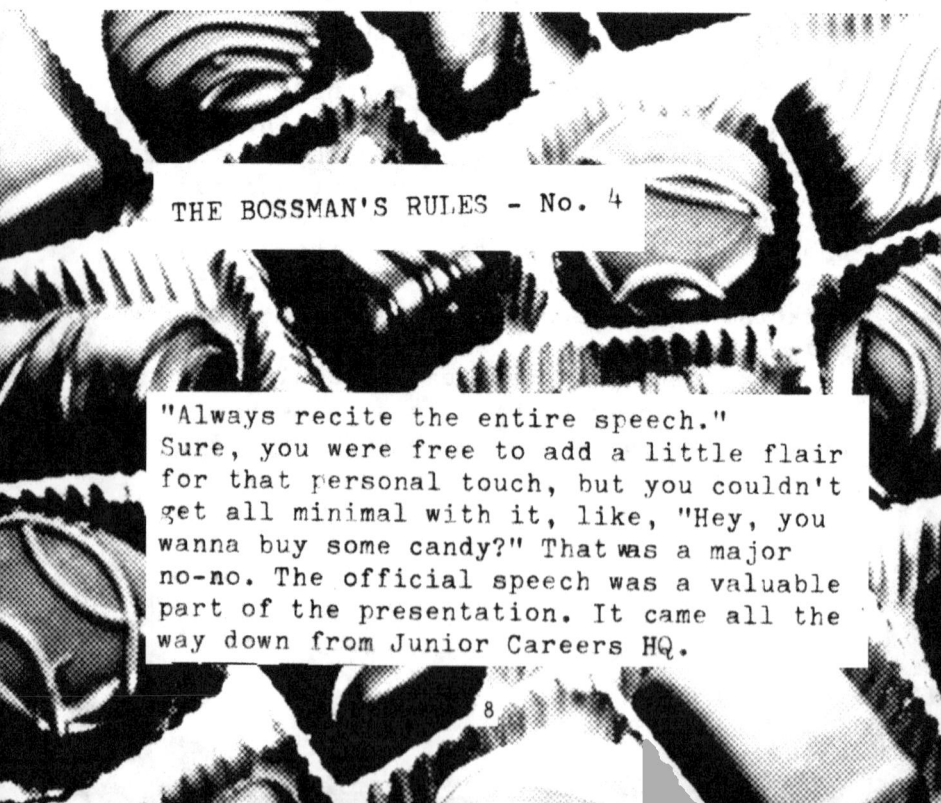

THE BOSSMAN'S RULES - No. 4

"Always recite the entire speech."
Sure, you were free to add a little flair
for that personal touch, but you couldn't
get all minimal with it, like, "Hey, you
wanna buy some candy?" That was a major
no-no. The official speech was a valuable
part of the presentation. It came all the
way down from Junior Careers HQ.

THE GOOD TALK

At each door, we recited our speech.
It wasn't hard to memorize. After the
first day, it was like the catchiest pop
song you'd ever heard. You couldn't get
it outa your head without a lobotomy.

"Hello, my name is Kelly and I work for
Junior Careers. Junior Careers is a non-
profit organization that helps kids twelve
to sixteen earn extra money and win
special trips. Right now I'm trying to win
a trip to Magic Mountain. I'd appreciate
you taking the time to look at some of the
items I have for sale."

At this point you were supposed to fall
to a knee and start removing candy from
the box.
"We got chocolate covered mint creams.
Fruit flavored hard candies. We got turtles,
and everybody's favorite: peanut brittle.
And, for the serious chocolate lover, our
top seller, delicious Belgian milk and
white chocolate swirled seashells."
The seashells weren't actually our top
seller, just the most expensive.

To make it with Junior Careers, you
couldn't be above a lie or two.

The way the Bossman put it, "An Earner
makes it happen. To get the customer in the
palm of your hand you gotta talk the good
talk. You gotta give them something to
believe in. Tell them a story. Tell them
anything. Just keep talking. If the person
thinks all they gotta do is say no, that's
what they're gonna do. You gotta give them
a reason to turn you down."

But the way I looked at it, when somebody
answered their door,and saw a kid standing
on their welcome mat with a box in his arms,
their minds were already made up.

They were either thinking, "Just what I
wanted! A tasty snack!"

Or, "How do I get rid of this punk without
getting on his bad side."

It was obvious.

Most people were cool.

"Sorry," they'd say politely after I
finished talking and give me the excuse
they'd been coming up with the whole time
I was delivering the spiel.

Some folks, though, could be downright
nasty, as if all I wanted to do with my
time was bug people while they're watching
the evening news.

Old fogies were the worst. They'd yell,
"No!" and slam the door in your face.

Of course, at that point, you had no
choice but to hawk a loogie on their
doorknob.

If you don't want people knocking on
your door, put up a No Soliciting sign.

For the door-to-door salesman the No
Soliciting sign is the same as a Beware of
Dog sign.

You just kept moving. *

─────────── THE BOSSMAN'S RULES - No. 5 ───────────

*This was the only time we were allowed
to break rule number five: "Never skip doors."

The Bossman always said, "Every door you knock on is another opportunity. The ones you skip, well... you'll never know. You know?"

Maybe he had a point. But sometimes it just didn't feel right.

Like when you came to a house and it was obvious people were dying a slow death inside. Or possibly already dead. Or when the house had too many steps. Or when you heard children crying and a woman screaming.

You couldn't help thinking about how pissed your own mother got when her interrupted her during a conniption fit with a simple question like, "When's dinner?"

So what's this lady, a complete stranger, gonna do if you start nagging her to buy some candy?

Sometimes it was better to just move on to the next place.

Or let your partner take the heat.

The Bossman sent us out in teams of two. We each had our own box of candy, but we shared a map of the route, a permit, and a piece of chalk.

As we worked our assigned territory, we marked the curbs with Xs, so the Bossman knew where we'd been and could find us when he returned later that evening to pick us up.

THE BOSSMAN'S RULES - No. 6

"Always mark your curbs." If the Bossman didn't see those Xs, he'd think you weren't covering all your territory and might dock your pay. More important though, if he had to drive the streets looking for, he'd get pissed as hell. And dock your pay for sure.

"Stay focused."
This was the hardest rule of them all.

When it came to partnering up, we always wanted to work with our friends. But the Bossman was no dummy. He knew that if we were having too much fun, we wouldn't get as much done.

There were always distractions.

Everywhere you went, the streets were filled with kids doing what kids did when they weren't in school. And there you were, lugging a box around like a chump.

Sometimes it seemed like every other kid in the world was having a blast except for you. It didn't matter that the Bossman said they were just being useless. You wanted in on the action as well.

THE STICK UP

When Gabe and I worked together we spent most of our time talking about the bands we were gonna start once we had enough money to buy guitars. Gabe was a metalhead like me. And not much of a seller either.

One night, in Arcadia, we were taking a smoke break on the curb, debating who the best shredder was, Yngwie Malmsteen or Randy Rhodes, when three white guys with a football approached us looking to start a pick-up game.

It was tempting, but we told them, "Can't.
We're working."

"Working?" one of the guys asked. "What
kind of job you got?"

"Selling candy."

"Candy?" The guys gathered around to
investigate the contents of our boxes.

"Let's have some."

Gabe and I exchanged a concerned glance.

These guys were bigger than us, but with
their bouffant 'dos and Izod shirts, it was
hard to be frightened.

"It's not ours to give away," I said.

"Yeah. We're supposed to sell it."

The guys thought about that and then said,
"So?"

"So?"

"So, if we don't sell it, we'll get in
trouble."

"With who? Your mommies?"

"No. Our boss."

"Man, fuck your boss."

This cracked up the other two guys. They
were all giggling like crazy, moving in
closer.

"C'mon, dudes," Gabe said as we grabbed
our boxes and backed away. "Be cool."

Sellers got jumped all the time. With that
big box of candy in your arms, you were an
easy target for a stick up. Gabe and I both
knew this. But we were in Arcadia, one of
those cities full of trees and grass--Most
of which were green. This confrontation was
more surprising than anything.

"It's not your shit, so what do you care?"

The third guy had a point. When faced with
a confrontation like this, your first instinct
would be to hand over the candy, but unless
you came back with a black eye, the Bossman
might hold you accountable for the lost
product.

"Give up the boxes or we'll just take them."

I looked at Gabe for the signal.

There was only one way out.

"Run!"

We hauled ass down the street. The guys
were right behind us. We were too scared

to turn around and see how close they were,
but we could hear their sneakers slap
against the concrete,

We ran as fast as our feet would take us,
bolting across lawns and through driveways.
We cut right. We cut left. But we couldn't
shake them. They were tight on our backs.

Just as we were about to dump our boxes
and split up, in the distance we heard the
familiar pattern of the Bossman's horn:
two shorts and a long.

We made a beeline for it.

When he saw us running with the pack of
guys behind us, the Bossman jumped out of the
van with the Louisville Slugger he kept
underneath his seat.

We ran behind him and faced off with the
guys. They weren't so ballsy up against a
home run hitter. They were still talking
shit, but maintained their distance.

"Get in the van!" shouted the Bossman.

We leapt over the front seat and into the
back. The Bossman got behind the wheel and
gunned the engine. As we peeled away, the
guys smacked the side of the van.

Gabe and I flipped them off through the
window.

"C'ya, muthafuckas!"

ASIDE NOTE

I started smoking with Gabe. One night, we were
taking a break and he pulled out a pack of
Marlboros. He was puffing and spitting so much,
I couldn't resist the offer to join in. But
the cigarette made me cough, and I got a major
headrush. I thought I was going to throw up.
Just as I was about to toss it in the gutter,
Gabe told me, his voice full of inspiration,
"You gotta keep trying, dude. Once you get the
hang of it, they taste awesome." So for the rest
of the evening, when Gabe lit up, I lit up.
And sure enough, by quitting time, I'd stopped
coughing. I was still dizzy, but from that day
on, I never looked back.

THE PERKS

We worked six days a week. On Saturdays,
we started first thing in the morning.
The days were long, but you almost always
made a nice chunk of change before the day
was over.

One Saturday David and I were working
the subdivisions of San Bernardino. From
one prefab house to the next. If we hadn't
been marking curbs, it woulda seemed like
we were covering the same territory.

When the cops pulled up and called us over
to the car, we were about to go into the
pitch, thinking they were looking to buy
some candy. But they wanted to see our
permits. We always carried these papers with
us, even though they'd been photocopied
so many times, they were practically
illegible. It was the first time we'd
ever been asked to show them. Turned out,
they weren't up to snuff. The cops put our
boxes in the trunk of the squad car and
told us to get in the backseat.

There were no cuffs, so we figured it
wasn't serious. We played it cool.

They drove us to the station, where the
rest of our crew were hanging out in a
large room.

Everybody was cracking jokes.

"Do you smell bacon?"

"I smell donuts."

"It sure smells like breakfast in here."

15

We knew they had no right to take us in.
We were just kids.

A few guys were worried, thinking the
Bossman might have left us high and dry.
Their dissent became contagious the longer
we waited. You couldn't help but wonder what
you would do if you were in his situation.
Most of us agreed, we'd get the fuck outa
dodge. Pronto.

But when we heard the Bossman's thunderous
voice outside the doors, and then saw him
burst into the room, we cheered and gathered
around him like he was Moses come to lead
us out of Egyptland.

Never doubted him for a moment!

As he tore into the cops for harassing
a bunch of underpriveledged kids trying
to make something of their lives, we
swore allegiance for all eternity.

"I got the permits!" he yelled, his voice
reverberating off the walls. "You can't
lock my kids up! I got the damn permits!"

In the end, the cops gave the Bossman a
ticket and told him never to come back to
San Berdoo.

"You don't hafta worry about that!"

While we walked to the van, we chanted,
"Donut! Donut!" over and over.

We were happy to be free, even though
our day was a bust. The sales had been
going really well that morning.

But the Bossman saved the day. Instead
of taking us home, he drove to Magic
Mountain and paid our way.

Musta rode every ride in the park.

After telling thousands of people that
we were working towards a trip there,
this was the first and only time we ever
went to Magic Mountain.

Not that there weren't other perks.

Once a month the Bossman had pool parties at his house in Diamond Bar.

He had a humongous pad. Two stories, TVs in every room, a jacuzzi and a pool. Sometimes he bought us beer and gave us rides on his Harley.

There were other benefits. Like, if you sold out your entire box during a shift you got a five dollar bonus. And at the end of each day, the kid with the highest sales got to ride up front and pick the radio station during the long ride home.

That was a luxury usually reserved for the Earners.

I always rode in the back of the van, where it smelled like stinky sneakers and BO. But it didn't matter.

You felt good when the workday was done. Especially with a couple bucks in your pocket.

As the picking-up process was reversed into the dropping-off, we sang along to the radio and told tales about all the crazy shit that had gone down on the route.

Some guy always had a wild story about this hot-to-trot chick answering the door half-naked. And you know, in pornos or in real life, those scenarios only lead to one thing. The closest I ever came to a random sexual encounter was when a girl in a low-cut blouse bent over to look in my box. Since she wasn't wearing a bra, I had a clear shot of her tits. They looked like bowling pins the way they hung off her chest.

That was the first time I'd seen live boobs that weren't related to me.

So I had no complaints.

El Monte was primo territory.

Especially on a Saturday morning, when the entire city seemed to be participating in the ritual of the day off.

The air was ripe with freshly-cooked chorizo and cheap pine cleansers. Shirts and pants and dresses hung from anything that could double as a clothesline.

While the women cooked and cleaned, the men worked on jalopies in the street.

Little kids rode their hand-me-down big wheels along the sidewalk, swerving to avoid empty beercans and shards of broken liquor bottles, the remnants of the week's paycheck.

Teenage vatos huddled like conspirators in alleyways.

And gaggles of young girls chirped away on patios, exchanging beauty tips and painting in their pencil-thin eyebrows.

Everybody was happy.

It was the perfect time to sell candy.

But as Juan and I made the rounds, lugging our boxes from one apartment complex to the next, I was striking out left and right.

PRIMO TERRITORY

One of the few whiteboys on the crew, I
was at a major disadvantage in the Mexican
neighborhoods. In the past, I had learned
an abbreviated version of the sales pitch,
so that if the person who answered the
door said, "No hablo Inglés," I could
respond with, "Quieres comprar dulces y
galletas?"

Except it didn't sound very Español coming
out of my mouth. No matter how much I
practiced, I couldn't get the hang of
rolling my Rs.

So my rendition sounded more like,
"Gettus compla dueces and gayetus?"

Even though most people got a kick out of
the blonde-haired, blue-eyed kid on their
doorstep speaking bad Spanish with a goofy
grin*, it was easy to say no when that was
the only word we had in common.

On the few occasions when a potential
customer had a question beyond my primitive
grasp of the language, I called Juan over
and he took the sale.

Juan was having a stellar day. One of the
top sellers on the crew, he almost always
rode up front. Dressed like a street urchin
in highwater slacks and a threadbare Polo
shirt, he was the master of the mercy sale.

Juan recited the speech in a whiny drawl
that could make a deaf person cringe.

All treble and no bass.

And he rarely took no for an answer.

He'd plead and cajole like a spoiled brat
until the person broke down and bought
something just to make him go away.

It was impressive, watching him work.
Even if each sale he made was another
reminder of how few I was making. Which,
as noon approached, came to a grand total
of none.

THE BOSSMAN'S RULES - No. 8

*"Always smile."

My lack of success amused Juan to no end.
Although he looked like a foresaken step-
child, Juan had the confidence of a royal
prince. When I asked for my cut of the
sales he'd swiped right from underneath
me, he was quick to point out that even if
I did speak Spanish, I'd never match him
as a salesman. He viewed my inability to
communicate with the locals as a character
flaw. And as the day progressed, I was too
weak from hunger to argue about it.

All I wanted was lunch. My stomach was
rumbling steady, With just one sale I'd
have enough for a McDonald's cheeseburger.
Of course, that would mean going home two
bucks in the hole, but it was better than
starving all day.

So I went through the motions, hoping
for a mercy sale of my own. Unfortunately,
"Gettus compla dueces and gayetus?" just
wasn't enough to close the deal.

I had lost all hope when we came to an
apartment building with a tropical island
theme, though the sun and fun of its original
design had long since faded into off
season squalor.

Juan suggested we split the floors. While
he went upstais, I started knocking on
doors on the first level.

"Gettus compla dueces and gayetus?"

"No. Lo siento."

I was 0 for fifteen when I got to the
last apartment.

It didn't look promising.

The windows pulsated from the beat of
Ranchero music blasting inside. Through
the door, I could clearly make out the
limpid accordian tune.

I assumed nobody would hear me, but I
knocked anyway. To my surprise, the door
swung open instantly and a burly man stood
in the doorway wearing a stained wife-beater.

A miasma of beer and cigarettes wafted from
the dank interior.

His pants were unbuckled and a belt dangled
in front of his crotch like a... like a...
like a limp dick.

I stumbled backwards as if I'd been
sucker-punched.

"Que?" the man asked as he bobbed and weaved to the incessant polka rhythm.

I was already walking away, but I paused long enough to shout over the music, "Gettus compla dueces and gayetus?"

"Que?" the man asked again lurching forward, his face yearning to understand.

I halted my retreat and raised my voice. "Gettus! Compla! Dueces! And! Gayetus!"

"Galletas?" the man shouted.

"Si" I bellowed. "Gayetus!"

"Quero galletas!" the man roared.

"Gayetus?" I asked and pulled out a box of butter cookies for his examination.

"Gettus compla?"

"Galletas!" The man smiled and grasped at the cookies. "Si!"

I pulled the box back and held up three fingers. Uno. Dos. "Tres dollarays." I knew my numbers, but I always had to start from the beginning.

The man looked confused for a moment, as if, in his beer-addled mind I was the cookie fairy going around passing out free cookies.

He almost lost his balance as he reached into his pocket and extracted a wad of cash.

His hands bulged from all the denominations, wrinkled and folded together, like a thick green ball. He was loaded.

Doubly loaded.

He pushed the unruly mess of bills on me and I picked through the twenties, tens and fives, until I found three singles.

Paid, I handed him the box of cookies.

"Galletas!" the man howled with rabid excitement. He ripped the box open as he stepped inside and slammed the door.

I weaved from the sudden silence.

"Galletas!" I said cheerfully to the empty courtyard, imitating his slurred pronunciation.

Not only had my Spanish improved, but I also had lunch money.

Next stop, McDonald's.

The Bossman would've lost his mind if he had
seen how the man was so blatantly snubbing his
nose at rule number nine: "Keep your money safe
and in order." The Bossman had a specific
method for managing the cash we collected on
our routes. Your bills had to be arranged by
denomination, all facing the same way.
"I want to see dead presidents looking at me
when I count your money at the end of the day."
If you tried to tell him that not all the dudes
on the bills had been presidents, he might
dock your pay for being a smartass. "And always
use a wallet." It was easy to lose your money
if you just shoved it in your pocket. And you
know for sure the Bossman would hold you
accountable for the difference if your count
was off at the end of the day.

I sat on the stairs and waited for Juan,
tapping my foot to the distant polka beat.
I chuckled to myself as I thought about
the drunk man.
If only there were more guys like that
in the world... I'd be on my way to the
top spot!
I started tapping my fingers against my
bouncing knee, retracing each step of the
sale... Oh man, that guy was fucked up!
I kept thinking about how wasted he was
when he held out all that cash... practically
giving it to me... He musta just got paid.
Struck it rich.
Or won the lottery.
Something...

Then it hit me.
When I pulled out those three dollars,
I coulda taken the whole wad.
Fuck!
The guy was so drunk, he wouldn't have
even known what happened.
Once he sobered up, he'd probably just
assume he lost it in the bars.
It woulda been the perfect crime!
Fuck!
There musta been a couple hundred!
At least!
Fuck!
Maybe even thousands!
Fuck!
Fuck!
Fuck!

I leapt to my feet and paced the courtyard,
kicking the plants that grew slipshod around
a sullen palm tree.
I'd just let the score of a lifetime fall
through my fingers. I could've retired from
Junior Careers right then and there with enough
money to buy all the junk food, magazines and
records I wanted.
At least for a little while.
But no! Stupid me. Stupid, stupid me...
In my excitement over finally making a sale,
all I was thinking about was a damn cheese-
burger.
Fuck!
When Juan came down the stairs, I hesitated
telling him about the lost windfall. But I
couldn't hold back my disappointment.
It all came out at once.
The drunk man.
The music.
The lack of English.
The box of cookies.
The wad of cash.

$ $ $ $

"Which apartment?" Juan demanded without hesitation.

"He already bought something," I pointed out. "How you gonna get him to buy more?"

"Leave it to me," Juan said, full of confidence. "This guy must be totally wasted if you sold him something. You don't even know what you're talking about. B esides, I can get anybody to but what I'm selling. Just watch and learn."

"Well, I better get a cut this time." I was thinking about all the other sales he'd made due to my verbal limitations.

Juan dismissed my claim with a wave of his hand and pounced on the door.

Just like the time before, as soon as he knocked, the door swung open and the drunk man stepped unsteadily onto the doormat, working his jaw slowly. In his hand was the ripped-open box of cookies.

Juan didn't miss a beat. He went right into the spiel. His high-pitched nasal voice was like a siren over the music.

He delivered the speech with all the embellishments that made him the superior salesman. Forceful and determined, Juan talked a mile a minute, not letting up on the pitch for even a breath.

I knew I was watching a master at work when he fell to his knees with a practiced bow and lifted up each item, extolling its potential culinary delight to the man, who weaved back and forth as he tried to keep an eye on the moving targets.

I couldn't understand much of what Juan was saying, but it sounded good.

It sounded professional.

Juan was going places. You could tell.

After he finished the speech, Juan waited patiently for a reply.

The man stood unfazed, like he hadn't heard a word Juan had just screamed in his face. The man swallowed the cookie he'd been chewing since he opened the door and reached into the box for another.

Undeterred, Juan went into another rant.

Still, the man said nothing. He just chewed the next cookie as slowly as the first.

Juan looked at the man. It was obvious he didn't know how to respond. He'd just given the man everything he had, exhausted every angle in his repetoire, all in the man's native tongue. And yet the man just only stood there, like a teetering statue.

Finally, his voice quivering with emotion, Juan made one last plea.

"Quieres comprar dulces y galletas?"

The man shoved his hand into the box and pulled out one of the round, sugar-coated cookies.

He held the cookie out to Juan.

"Tu queres?"

Juan stood frozen until the man shoved the cookie into his mouth and slammed the door.

THE BOSSMAN'S RULES - No. 10

Later, in a booth at McDonald's, we started to laugh. However tragic it may have been that we hadn't been able to get the drunk man's loot, Juan had to admit we had one helluva story for the guys back in the van that night. And there was still rule number ten to consider. The Bossman always said, "No matter how bad things seem, never give up." There were plenty more sales out there. For the Earners who knew how to make it happen. And the Useless, if you got lucky.

PILTDOWNLAD NO. 3

Fucked up and photocopied by Irina Dessaint

This story began as an anecdote about how I started
smoking. But I couldn't write about working as a
candy salesman without mentioning the drunk Mexican
incident. Or the time a bunch of preps tried to
jump me in Arcadia. From there, the story mushroomed
into a jumbled collection of all my memories
working for Junior Careers. And since I have so
many memories from that period of my life, the end
result is a long and meandering story. There is no
real core structue and, as one critic put it,
"nothing at stake." Somebody else commented that
there are two stories and that only the second one
("Primo Territory") is cohesive. Which begs the
question, Why force the reader to plow through a
slew of facts and incidental remembrances to get
at the real story?

I don't know. But in my old neighborhood, almost
everybody worked for Junior Careers at one point or
another. Unless you got an allowance from your folks
you had to work for the things you wanted. And there
really weren't any other jobs for the under-sixteen
set. The smarter guys realized they were getting
exploited and quit after a few days. I stuck at if
for over a year.

Selling candy door-to-door as a troubled twelve
and thirteen year old was a pivotal episode in my
childhood--my first taste of freedom. Not only was
I earning a little pocket money, I also had an excuse
to leave my crazy house each day, something I'd been
trying to do since I figured out I could ride my
bike past the four block radius of my neighborhood.
With Junior Careers, I went to so many different
parts of town, met and talked with so many different
people, and worked alongside all sorts of kids from
a variety of backgrounds. These were the halcyon
days of my youth and I wanted to commemorate
the whole experience. But anyway, you should feel
free to skip through the first part and only read
the last story. It's the one I always tell when I
tell the story of my stint as a door-to-door
candy salesman.

PILTDOWNLAD

№ 3

"The never-ending dread that he'll never actually make enough money to keep any in his pocket after paying the boss for all the candy he eats is hilariously devastating." - Razorcake

"Kelly's direct writing style draws the reader into the scene and immerses you in that time and place -- I can almost feel the sidewalks beneath my feet and hear the bossman growling."
                                        - DJ Frederick

"I'm really tired of reading about people's shitty jobs. This is still pretty funny though... Man, it sounds like that job sucked." - Maximum Rocknroll

THE GÜERO CHINGÓN STORIES

PILTDOWNLAD #1

"The Guero Chingon Stories"

Vol. 1

These stories were originally published as individual micro-zines (2.75 x 4.25) under the title "Guero Chingon" and distributed around downtown LA during the summer of 2011. They were written on my Olympia but transcribed into InDesign. I printed fifty to one hundred of each issue and attributed them to "Piltdownlad." When that name went from a pseudonym to the name of the zine, the five Guero Chingon issues became Piltdownlad #1. They are collected here with a new introduction.

(c) 2011, 2012
Written on an Olympia De Luxe manual by Kelly Dessaint

Illustrations by Art Mark

Cover and title graphics by Irina Dessaint

INTRODUCTION

I was born on the San Bernardino Freeway. East-
bound side. A twelve-foot concrete wall separated
my backyard from the fury of transportation on one
of the busiest freeways in LA: six lanes going east,
six lanes going west, and down the center, the Union
Pacific. Behind the wall, traffic was a constant
roar. During rush hour, the cars crept by slowly,
with faulty mufflers sputtering, transmission grinding, gears shifting, engine blocks rattling, brakes
squealing and stereos blasting. Motorcycles main-
lined as sedans idled. Eighteen-wheelers struggled
in low gear. The occasional clunker stalled on the
shoulder. Frantic voices shouting into the call box
phone. At night, the cars came in waves. In the ebb
and flow of late night transit, there were moments
of silence, and in those brief periods of calm, I
discovered infinity, like a strip of gauze stretched
taut.
  My folks bought the two-bedroom house in Rosemead
the same year I was born, 1971. It was conveniently
located exactly eleven miles from the bank downtown

where the old man worked. Each morning he got on the
freeway and made the westbound commute. Later, he
took a full-time position at the Army reserve center
in El Monte, a few miles east on the freeway. When
he split the scene with mom, he got an apartment in
Baldwin Park, a little further down the freeway.
And after my little brother and I moved in with him
and then left for Alabama, we took the freeway all
the way to Texas before it split into I-20. Coulda
gone straight to Florida, that's how long and mighty
that freeway is. From sea to shining sea...

Even though it wasn't exactly a barrio, in the 70s,
Rosemead and the surrounding area were predominantly
Chicano. If you called it East LA, only the nit-
pickers would argue. Rosemead was gang territory.
Our street belonged to Lomas. The other side of the
freeway was Sangra turf. Although the gangs weren't
very active anymore--everybody in jail, too old or
shot up to fight like the good ole days--signs
of the old rivalries were omnipresent. Almost every
available wall, fence, post and curb was covered in
chicken scratch graffiti. We knew the chips in the
stucco of our house were from stray Sangra bullets
aimed at our neighbor, Joker, who used to hide in our
crawlspace when the cops came looking for him.
Joker was always cool to us. We were proud to have
been born in Lomas territory, but the kids, the
wannabe vatos, they never let us forget we were
different. Sure, there were some old white people
around and the occasional half-breed, but on our
street, we were the only white family. And we weren't
just white: we were tow-headed, blue-eyed, lilywhite
Mormons. The burgeoning cholos regarded us with
complete didain. Sometimes they called us Children
of the Corn, but mostly they referred to us as
the gueros.

From the first day of school, we weren't just
bullied, we were brutalized. With my babyface and
big mouth, I was such a target of contempt, I had
to start running fifteen seconds before the final
bell just to make it out the door without a fare-
well knuckle sandwich. It got so bad, our folks sent
us to the Y to learn karate. But the classes were on
Friday nights, same time as Dukes of Hazard and
Dallas. I didn't see why I had to miss my favorite
TV shows on account of some assholes who didn't like
me because I was born with such loathsome features

as blond hair and blue eyes. Besides, I wasn't much of a fighter. Self-defense wasn't my thing. So I learned to run faster. And talked shit like there was no tomorrow.

After a particularly violent beatdown, when some kids knocked me off the jungle gym and stomped my balls until I went into convulsions (if I ever have kids and they come out deformed, I'll know who to blame), the folks finagled a way to send us all to a school in Alhambra. But things weren't much better there. The upper middle-class kids knew we didn't belong. We had the stink of poverty and ridicule on us. And they had their own methods of keeping the weaker kids down. Most of our classmates weren't allowed to hang out with us after school because when they did, we took them panhandling or set garbage cans on fire. One kid fell off the freeway wall and impaled his leg on the spikes of a chainlink fence. His father threatened to sue, but let it go when he realized we had nothing to take. We were pariahs. White trash. So in the afternoons, we were back on the street, where the neighborhood guys made us pay a hefty toll to ride our bikes and play games on their turf.

By the time the folks split up the summer before I started high school, it hardly mattered that I was going back to public school. I knew there was no escape from the hazing. It was part of my identity. My only recourse was to act like I didn't mind getting ragged on, and to prove I was just as tough as anybody else from Rosemead.

THE PILLSBURY CHOLO

Hector wanted to look tough. With his hair slicked back, the bandana low on his forehead, the pressed chinos and the plaid shirt buttoned at the collar, he was the epitome of cholo severity. But no matter how chingon he dressed, Hector had a face like the Pillsbury doughboy. His chubby cheeks pushed up the sides of his mouth into a permanent grin, so that, regardless of his mood, he was always smiling. To compensate for this cheerful countenance, Hector did all he could to boost his cred and prove what a badass he really was.

In fourth period wood shop at Mark Keppel High, I watched Hector run circles to impress the homeboys in class. He was non-stop talking shit, bragging about the many heinas he'd banged or the five Sangra locos he took on all by himself. Everybody knew he was full of shit, but his uncle was a big shot in Lomas, doing time for attempted murder in Pelican Bay, so they played along out of respect.

As the only white guy in shop class, I was an easy target for a bully like Hector. The verbal taunts started at the beginning of the semester.

"Yo, guero. Weren't you at the bowling alley the other night?"

"No, what are you talking about?"

"Oh, musta been some other guero. You whiteboys all look the same to me."

Hahahahaha.

It was all fun and games until the day I walked into the classroom just as Hector turned the corner and shoulder-blocked me. I wasn't expecting the sudden impact and fell backwards. "What the fuck!"

Hector sniggered into his fist as he sauntered away. "Sorry, homes. Didn't see you there."

At first, I couldn't gauge the sincerity in his apology since his perma-smile was the ultimate poker face. So I let it slide. But a few weeks later, just as I was about to take my seat in class, Hector pulled the stool out from under me. I managed to grab the edge of the work table before my ass hit the ground.

6

"Oh, were you gonna sit there?" Hector asked in a high-pitched mocking tone. "Sorry, eh."

"He's punking you, ese," Sergio told me later, as we shared the belt-sander. "If you keep taking his shit, you'll be his bitch forever."

Sergio had a point. It seemed like I'd been in the crosshairs of one mental midget thug after another my whole life. I'd always taken the high road before, but now that I was in high school, I didn't want to spend the next four years getting pushed around by a fat bastard like Hector. So I asked Sergio, "What can I do?" Sergio lived down the street from me. His mom bought Avon from my mom. Sergio was truly chingon... to the bone. I once saw him beat the shit out of a guy without even using a fist. He just grabbed the dude by the ears and slammed his face into his knee. Over and over, until his pantleg was crimson.

"You gotta duke him, vato. Right in his goofy mouth. One blow. That's all it takes. The fat boys always go down easy. Trust me."

I wanted to believe Sergio. He'd always been cool to me. But Hector was twice my weight class. I wouldn't have gambled on my odds. Even though I never missed an episode of WWF wrestling, I doubted any of the moves I tried out on my little brother would help me when it came to throwing blows for real. Still, I had to do something...

About a week later, back in shop class, Hector was eating sunflower seeds at the next table over. As he cracked them open between his snaggled teeth, he flicked one of the moist shells onto my arm. I turned and glared.

Hector was all smiles. "Que pasa, homes? Want some polly seeds?"

I ignored his offer and went back to work. Earlier, when I got to class, I had found a strip of nails for the shop nailgun under my table. There were about fifteen nails in a row. Like a serrated blade. As I flipped the nails over in my hand, the razor sharp edge nicked my thumb. When a second shell landed on my arm, I stood up and felt the sweat of my palm against the strip of nails. "Knock it off, asshole!" I shouted.

7

My protest sent Hector into a fit of laughter.
"Orale!" He slapped his seatmate's shoulder and
said, loud enough for the whole class to hear, "Check
out guero chingon!"

I glanced across the room towards the teacher who
was helping a student file a block of wood. His back
was turned, oblivious as ever. It was now or never.
I reared back, Fernando Valenzuela style, and chucked
the strip of nails right at the fat motherfucker.

In the red light haze of fury, I heard a wail and
opened my eyes. I didn't even realize I'd squeezed
them shut until the scene came into focus. Hector
was clutching his forearm. A torrent of blood gushed
through his fingers and collected in the sawdust.
He looked like a maniacal laughing clown, his lips
forming a smile, even in pain.

I was immediately collared and escorted to the
principal's office, where they read me the riot act:
"Your attendance record is dreadful, your grades
a disgrace, and now this... You've left us with no
other choice but expulsion."

I phoned the old man at the reserve center and
waited across the street, smoking and fantasizing
about my new life of leisure. When the old man pulled
up, still in his Army fatigues, he said, "I guess I
need to go in there and sort this crap out."
"It's no use," I told him. "They said I gotta go."
But he went anyway and testified on my behalf.
"He's really a good kid... things are rough for him
at home... his mother's never around... there's no
discipline... as soon as I get custody he'll be
living in a new school district, so if he could only
finish out the year..."
Of course they bought his spiel. Nothing like a hard
luck tale from a man in uniform. Shit, with all those
stripes and chevrons on his shoulders, the old man
outranked most authority figures. He'd gotten us out
of more than one tight spot with his military status
in the civilian world.
My sentence was reduced to a week's suspension and
for the rest of the year I had to carry an attendance card to prove I'd been to class. So there was no
more ditching after lunch to hang out with the stone-
ers at 7-Eleven. But it was a small price to pay.
From that day on, thanks to Hector, I was known as
Güero Chingon.

Joey and I were hanging out at the Sav-On plaza, like we did most days that summer. I was sitting on the small firetruck that jerked back and forth, while Joey straddled the silver pony that bounced up and down. But the rides were idle. Even if we had been flush, a quarter was too precious to waste on a few minutes of mechanical jostling. Instead, we killed time watching the shoppers come and go.

It seemed like the whole world was out spending money except for us. We had needs too, but once Baby Sister showed up on the scene, allowances were a thing of the past. Room and board, that's all we got anymore. For everything else, we were on our own.

Once school let out, we tried any way we could to make a buck. We hit up the neighbors, looking to do odd jobs. But what could we do? We were kids. We had no skills. Some folks took pity on us. We swept a few driveways and weeded a couple gardens. The junkman once hired us to haul a mysterious pile of bricks from the front of his house to the back. Paid us a dollar each. Rick was good for a quarter or two, but only if we helped him jack off.

For a while, we tried collecting bottles for the deposit, thinking we'd make a fortune for sure. Bottles were three cents a pop and people threw them away like they were trash. So one morning, we snagged a shopping cart and pushed it all around the neighborhood picking up empties. But after scrounging through slop-filled garbage cans for several hours, we took our bounty to the store and cashed out. All we got was a lousy seventy-five cents. Split down the middle. A total bust. Too much work for too little profit. There had to be an easier way.

Then we discovered panhandling. We were hanging out in front of the Alpha-Beta one day and I double-dared Joey to ask a lady walking into the store for a dime. Joey never turned down a dare. Especially a double dare. He walked right up to her and said, "Excuse me, ma'am. Do you have a dime so I can call my mom?"

I had a grin the size of a pothole when I saw the lady stop, open her change purse and place a shiny coin in his palm.

It was like a miracle, that first taste of free money. We spent the rest of the day with our feet on the pad that opened the sliding doors, our hands held high, asking all who entered, "Excuse me, do you have a dime?"

When the manager chased us off, we moved on to the next place of business. Over the next few weeks, we must have covered every grocery, restaurant, liquor store and bar in Rosemead, Monterey Park, San Gabriel, Alhambra and parts of Temple City. We went anywhere we knew adults would be spending money. Worked like a charm, until Mrs. Garcia spotted us outside the Post Office. She told mom and that was the end of that racket.

11

So there we were, on the skids, sitting on the
rides that never went anywhere, as the world of
commerce streamed past, when Nate happened by.

He didn't even say hello, just went straight up to
the row of newspaper boxes. We joined our brother
where he stood, looking at the front page of the
LA Times.

"Whatcha doing, Nate?"

"You ever thought about how a newspaper box works?"

Joey and I shook our heads. Only Nate thought
about things like that.

"It's quite simple, really. You put a quarter in
the slot and it slides through a mechanism that un-
locks the door. Then it falls into this compartment
right here under the handle." Nate tapped the silver
metal plate on the front of the box. "Must be a ton
of quarters in there."

Joey and I shrugged. "So?"

"So, you probably think it's impossible to get
them out, right?"

Joey and I nodded.

"Well, check it out." Nate dropped a coin into the slot and lifted the door. "You see this hole right here." He pointed to a square opening inside the box, next to where the papers were stacked. "If my calculations are correct, this hole leads to the compartment where the quarters are."

Joey and I looked at a hole too small for any hand. "Okay. So what?"

"Lemme see your gum," Nate told Joey, who spit out the wad of Juicy Fruit he'd been gnawing on since breakfast.

Nate pulled a straw from his pocket and mashed the gum onto the end of it. We eagle-eyed his technique as he lowered the straw, gum-end, into the hole and circled it around slowly. When he pulled the straw out, stuck to the wad of gum like fish on a hook, were two quarters, sparkling in the sunlight.

"Fucking NateGyver!" Joey and I patted him on the back, ecstatic. "That was awesome!"

"Be cool." Nate scanned the parking lot. "Don't wanna attract too much attention. Now here's the deal."

Nate began issuing instructions. Joey went into the drug store to buy a pack of Bubblicious with one of the newly acquired quarters while I searched the ground for straws.

"The thicker the better," Nate said. "Look for the ones from McDonald's."

When Joey got back with the gum, Nate put him on lookout and we went to work. Slowly, we extracted the quarters, two and three at a time. After we cleaned out the Times box, we moved on to the Examiner, followed by the Tribune.

Once all the boxes were empty, we counted our loot in the alley behind the store. Seventeen bucks even. And two slugs. Split three ways, our pockets bulged and jangled as we headed to Jim's to celebrate.

We placed our orders and laid the stacks of quarters on the counter. The woman at the register said, "What'd you boys do, break open your piggybanks?"

"That's right!" I slapped Nate's shoulder. "It's our brother's birthday and we're treating him to a feast."

"In that case," she said. "Here's a sundae on the house."

The next afternoon, Joey and I were geared up to hit the newspaper boxes at the Boy's Market on Del Mar. "They got a whole bunch over there," we told Nate. "Think of all the quarters we could score!"

But Nate was over it. "That's chump change. I got a better idea. You know the old junkman? Well, I got it on authority that he's got this massive stash of silver dollars. I'm talking pickle jars full of them. Keeps them in his closet. And get this, my source tells me that sometime this weekend he'll be cruising out to San Bernardino, where his wife is planted. Think about it. This is the perfect time to make a move. I could use a couple lookouts. We'll split the take three ways. Just like last time. What d'ya say? You guys down for a real heist?"

"Guess who I saw today," Oscar said as he rumma-
ged through the kitchen cupboards, checking each
package of ramen for his favorite, shrimp. At first
I thought it was an off-handed comment, but when he
answered his own question with, "Your best friend,
Eddie," I nearly choked. Just the mention of Eddie's
name and my guts clenched up like a fist.

"So?" I pretended not to give a shit.

Oscar found the flavor he was looking for, smacked
the bag against the counter and ripped it open.
"Tell your mom to get more shrimp. This is the last
one."

"So what did he say?" I asked casually, even though the suspense was killing me.

"Oh, he said your ass is grass the next time he sees you." Oscar laughed and poured the flavor packet over the shattered noodles.

"He said that?" It came out as an unanticipated squeak.

"Dude, you never shoulda messed with him." Oscar grinned wide as he shook the bag. "So he doesn't like cats. What's it to ya?"

Oh, the injustice of it all... Earlier that day, I was sitting on my porch when Eddie walked by and kicked my cat. Completely unprovoked. Fluffy was just minding his own business, sunbathing on the sidewalk. After he screeched across the yard, I went over to the fence and said, "Hey, man. Don't kick my cat." That's all. Next thing I knew, I was on the ground. Didn't even see Eddie make a fist before I saw stars. "Motherfucker," I seethed when I came to a few seconds later. I jumped up and ran inside my house to grab the aluminum bat I kept with my old little league gear in the living room. I charged outside, ready to rumble. Eddie saw me coming and took off. I chased after him, swinging the bat over my head like a barbarian raider, shouting, "Come back here so I can bash your fucking brains in!" By the time I reached the corner, he was a distant figure. "MOTHERFUCKER!"

16

Later that afternoon, as I held a sandwich bag of
ice against my shiner, Oscar showed up. He lived
down the street but made daily pit-stops
at our house to pillage our well-stocked cupboards. Mom usually made sure we had plenty of snack
foods to tie us over until dinner. When he told me
that Eddie was on the warpath, I tried to save face
behind a veil of bravado.

"Fuck Eddie. I'm ready to throw blows anytime.
Lucky for him he ran away like a yellow-bellied
homo. Otherwise, I woulda fucked him up." I picked
up the bat and hit my palm with the business end for
emphasis. "Big time."

"Stupid. You can't carry that bat around with you
everywhere you go." Oscar tapped the bottom of his
ramen bag to make sure he'd gotten all the crumbs
and mumbled, "Besides, he'll just take it away from
you and shove it up your culo."

"Yeah, right."

"Just watch. One day you'll be walking home from
school and you won't even see it coming. He'll be
like the Predator." Oscar cracked up at his joke.
As if he sensed my growing dismay, he added, "Course,
you could just say you're sorry."

"Really?" I raised my eyebrows at the prospect.
"You think?"

"Sure. I mean, he's still gonna duke you, but at
least you'll get it over with."

"Oh, man."

Oscar laughed so hard he spewed ramen dust across
the table.

In retrospect, I probably shouldn't have challen-
ged Eddie's right to kick my cat. He was a real thug.
Long after the rest of us had given up the fantasy
of being as buff as Lou Ferrigno and Arnold Schwar-
zenegger, Eddie kept pumping iron. He played football
at Keppel and walked like he was about to fall backwards. Convinced by Oscar that a showdown was inevitable, I went on high-alert. For the next few weeks,
I avoided certain streets and took the long way to
the corner store. Day and night, I maintained a
roving eye for any potential ambush. I walked with a
lit cigarette, in case I had to stub it out in
Eddie's eye to make a getaway. But after a month had

gone by, I began to think I could dodge Eddie indef-
initely. Despite the occasional update from Oscar,
all was quiet in the neighborhood.

I'd almost forgotten about Eddie when I walked outside one day and saw Oscar and some of the poppers
and lockers from down the street breakdancing
on the sidewalk in front of my house. I was pissed.
This was rocker turf, and they knew it.

Without thinking, I went out the gate and approached the group. One guy was spinning on his hand while
the other four crouched along the edge of the cardboard watching and egging him on.

"Hey!" I shouted. "You can't do that shit on my property!"

"Fuck you," said Oscar. "This is city property."

"I don't give a fuck. You gotta go!"

"You gonna make us?" asked a guy whose back was to me. When he turned around, I felt a gob of panic lodged in my throat.

"Where's your bat now, motherfucker?"

Before I could run back into my yard, Eddie and the breakers surrounded me. I glanced at their smiling, menacing faces and heard the snap, crack and pop of sweaty knuckles. I thought of my trusty bat, leaning against the wall by the front door.

"C'mon, dudes. Be cool." I made a move to break free from the pack, but they instantly grabbed my wrists and shoulders.

"Not so fast, guero," said Eddie. "You're coming with us."

They pushed me into the street.

"Where we going?" I asked. "Your sister on the clock? Seriously, man. I'm cool. I hit that shit last week and I'm still sick to my stomach. Tell your old man I want my nickel back."

Before I could laugh, Eddie nailed me in the back while another guy slapped my head.

"Hold him tight!" Oscar shouted. With a running start, he kicked me right in the ass crack. I fell down and winced as the rough asphalt bit into my hands.

"Yuck it up now, funny boy." Oscar set off a real laugh riot among his friends.

"That all you got?" I groaned. "Fucking beaners!"

I lunged towards my fence, but Eddie twisted my arm and put me in a headlock. When I struggled, he squeezed tighter.

Bent over, like a heretic in stocks, I looked up at Oscar. "Fuck you, Oscar Meyer, dick dog. You better not come to my house no more."

"Fuck your nasty house. You're getting what's coming to you. I always told you that big mouth of yours was gonna get your ass kicked one day."

I took a few punches and then one of the breakers said, "No, no, I got a better plan."

They huddled and busted up laughing.

"Yeah!"

"Time to pay up, motherfucker."

I was at their mercy. I knew it. There was nothing I could do as they marched me up the street but unleash a fusillade of invectives:

"YOU COCKSUCKING MOTHERFUCKING WETBACK FAGGOT ASS FAGGOTS CUM BREATHERS SONS OF BITCHES WHORES FOR MOTHERS BUTT FUCKING HOMOS I BET YOU FUCK EACH OTHER UP THE ASS EVERY NIGHT WITH YOUR TINY LITTLE DICKS!!!"

Eddie tightened his hold on my windpipe to shut me up and I made the rest of the journey up the hill struggling to stay on my feet.

At the end of the street, Eddie released the chokehold and pushed me onto the freeway ramp. I glanced across the sea of ivy at the speeding cars. Without the wall to block the noise, the sound of traffic was a cacophonous roar.

"What the fuck?" I asked.

"You only got one way to go." Eddie pointed at the freeway entrance. The others laughed.

"Really?" Now it was my turn to smile. "You want me to get on the freeway?" Suckers. Little did they know, I grew up with the fury of transportation in my backyard. The freeway was my Mississippi.

Casually, I straightened the wrinkles in my t-shirt from being twisted in their fists and said, "You know what? Fuck you and your cum-gurgling whore mothers!" I let out a long-winded kamikaze cry and took off down the ramp.

I ran along the shoulder of the freeway as the cars and trucks whizzed by. Some honked, to let me know I was in danger. I stayed close to the wall, keeping an eye on the ground for any jetsam or tufts of weeds protruding from the broken patches of asphalt. As I passed my house, I recognized the tree branches hanging over the wall. I kept going. The wall was twice my height. There was no way I could climb over. But under the pedestrian bridge, there was a section of the wall that was shorter than the rest. That's where I scaled the rough-hewn brick surface and dropped into the ivy. To avoid a confrontation with the breakers, I headed for a narrow passageway along the wall that led through my neighbors' backyards. I jumped a few fences and landed safe and sound in my own backyard.

As I passed the lemon tree, I smiled. I'll show
those motherfuckers, I thought. I made a basket with
my shirt and filled it with fruit. I climbed onto the
roof of my house and waited.

When I heard their voices I took aim.

"FUCK YOU FAGGOT WETBACK MOTHERFUCKERS!!!!"

As I chucked the lemons, I was screaming and laughing so hard I almost fell off the roof. Under the
onslaught of citrus missiles, the breakers ran
serpentine. By the time I exhausted my arsenal, they
had scattered.

"Don't forget your stupid cardboard!" I yelled into
the empty street.

The next day, Javier stopped by my house. He lived
down the street, in the same duplex as Oscar. After
pouring himself a glass of Kool-Aid, he said, "I
heard about your chingasa with Oscar and Eddie."

"Yeah. I really showed them, didn't I?" I had been
all smiles since.

"You know, you're only making shit worse for yourself. You need to mellow out."

"Fuck them!"

"You just don't get it, do you?"

"What's to get? They're assholes."

"Let me see if I can explain this so you'll understand..." Javier tossed the plastic cup in the sink
and wiped off a red moustache. "You remember how in
Scarface the guy ended up with no allies in the end,
so when the assassins came for him, he was all alone?
Well, you're like that. You got no friends on the
street. Everybody thinks you're a dick. I think you're
a dick. If it weren't for your brother Nate I wouldn't
even be talking to you about this."

I considered his advice. "So what you're saying
is that I'm like Tony Montana?" I assumed a machine-
gun wielding pose and said in my best Cuban accent,
"Fuck with me, you fucking with the best."

"Stupid. I'm just trying to help." Javier turned
to leave.

"Hey, Javie."

"What?"

"Say goodbye to the bad guy."

Alfonso was a major pyro. He was always playing
with matches and starting small blazes around the
neighborhood. I was into fire too, so even though
he was three years younger than me, we'd hang out
sometimes and burn things.

When the Herrera family moved out of the house
down the street, Alfonso and I were the first ones
on the scene. Through the windows, we looked at the
junk they'd left scattered across the floor. Figuring there had to be something worth salvaging, we
found an unlocked window and Alfonso crawled in to
open the back door. After sifting among the out-
dated newspapers and empty boxes, all we scored were
a couple videocassettes. The labels were in Spanish.

"Hey, Alfie. What's this say?"

"How am I supposed to know?"

"Don't you speak wetback?"

"Chinga tu madre."

"Is that a good movie?"

Alfonso walked into the kitchen and stood at the
stove. He tried the knob and after a hiss and a snap,
the burner flickered to life. "Oh, looky here."

We hovered before the blue flame like conjurers
around a black cauldron.

"Check it out." I pulled out some tape from one
of the videocassettes and held it over the burner.
Instantly, the thin strip recoiled from the heat and
incinerated into the air like black snowflakes.

"Cool!" Alfonso enthused. "Let me have some too."

Once the tape was gone, we moved on to milk cartons
and sandwich bags. Then I had a brilliant idea.

"What if we stuff the oven with all this crap
around here and then..."

"Set it on fire?"

22

"Stupid. No, we turn the oven on full blast."
"Then what?"
"Then KABLAMO!"
"You really think it'll explode?"
"Fuck yeah. It's gonna blow this whole house
straight up into the sky. And then it's gonna come
crashing down--BOOM! Like a nuclear bomb!"
"A nuclear bomb?"
"Even better--An oven bomb!"
"This is gonna rule!"
"Oven bomb!" we chanted. "Oven bomb!"
As the Looney Tunes scenario played out in our
heads, we collected all the paper, cardboard, plastic
and glass we could fit inside the oven. When it was
full, we turned the knob to five hundred.
"RUN!"
We charged out of the house and waited across the
street for the massive explosion we thought for sure
would take out half the block, if not the entire
city. But after fifteen minutes passed and nothing
had happened, we started to get restless.
"When's it gonna blow?" asked Alfonso.
"Who knows. Why don't you go in and find out."
"No way! I'm not going in there."
"Pussy."
"You do it then."
"I'm not the one with ants in my pants."
"I can wait."
"Me too."
So we waited.
And we waited.
Then it started to get dark. The Munsters was
about to come on TV and seeing as how the oven bomb
was a dud, I said, "This is lame. I'm going home."
Half an hour later, as the credits rolled, I heard
sirens in the distance. Getting louder. I went out-
side and looked toward the vacant house. Gray smoke
was billowing from the window we'd left open.
"Holy shit! It worked!"
I ran down the sidewalk and stood across from the
house. The sirens reached a crescendo when a fire
engine screamed onto our street, followed by a para-
medic truck. I mingled among the crowd of gawkers
watching the firemen work. It was like Emergency 51,
with red lights flashing and firemen shouting into
walkie-talkies. A crew pulled the hose down the drive-

way and aimed a geyser through the front door of the
house. In less than two minutes, the smoke was reduced
to steam. Several firefighters dragged the blackened
stove into the yard. I crossed the street to get a
better view. Unbelievably, the inside of the house
was hardly burned.

So the oven didn't explode after all, I thought.
Bummer.

Since the crowd was breaking up, I headed home. I
was about to unlatch my gate when I noticed Alfonso
on the sidewalk with his mother. She was holding him
up by the arm, his feet barely touching the ground.
Spanish firecrackers popped from her mouth. I watched
with dread as his free arm slowly raised and pointed
right at me.

Busted.

The asswhipping that night was set to the beat of
"YOU! WILL! NOT! START! FIRES!" The tune was fifty
lashes.

"You're lucky nobody got hurt," the old man said,
as he buckled his tortue device.

I rubbed my ass and thought about saying somebody
had, but figured it was better to keep my mouth shut.

Two weeks later, my first piece of business as a
free man was to get even with Alfonso for ratting
me out. I hid behind Mrs. Garcia's wooden fence
until Alfonso walked past. I jumped out and tackled
the fink onto the grass.

"Motherfucker!" I rubbed his face in the turf
until he was sobbing.

"I had no choice!" he cried. "She was gonna beat
me! She knew I'd done it. She knew!"

"Still, you shoulda kept your mouth shut."

"I'm sorry," he whimpered. His cheeks were plastered with tear-streaked mud and flecks of grass. He
looked so pathetic, I felt bad for roughing him up.
Had I been in his position, I probably would've done
the same thing. As a peace offering, I gave him the
book of matches I'd swiped from the old man's Pinto.

"They're yours. Tomorrow we'll go up to the ivy
and blaze. Cool?"

Alfonso snuffled the last gob of snot and smiled.
"Okay."

The next day, I waited behind the junkman's mag-
nolia for Alfonso to make an appearance. "ALFIE!"
I yelled several times, mindful to stay under cover
in case his mother was around. Finally, his older
brother came to the door.

I emerged from my hiding place. "Where's Alfonso?"
"He can't come out and play," Umberto said. "He's
grounded."

"What'd he do this time?"

"Same-o, same-o. He got two days."

From the side of the house, I saw Alfonso lean
his head out a window. "Hey!" he yelled. "I can't
come out!"

I laughed. "Sucks to be you!"

Alfonso flipped me off and held up the book of
matches I'd given him.

"You better wait for me!" I shouted. "Those are
half mine."

He pulled a match out and struck it. Smiling, he
let it burn between his fingers.

"So what?" I changed my tactic and acted as though
the loss of the matches didn't bother me at all.

Alfonso lit another match.

"Burn all you want! More where those came from."

I stood in front of his house for a while, pointing and laughing at his predicament, until I got
bored and wandered off.

Later that afternoon, I was digging up mom's flower-
beds to make a bunker for my Fischer-Price action
figures, when I smelled smoke. I looked up and down
the street. It was coming from Alfonso's house.

"That fucker!"

I took off to see what he'd ignited without me.
Outside his gate, I stood dumbfounded as I watched
a giant plume of smoke undulating from the back of
the house, as if a hundred barbeques were going at
once.

Next door, the junkman was yanking on his garden
hose. "I already called the fire department," he
told me. "Help me untangle this hose."

"Did Alfonso and his brother get out?" I asked as
I ran into his yard.

"I don't know."

We got the old, crusty hose loose, but it was too
short and the water pressure wasn't strong enough to
make it past the rose bushes along his fence. Not that
it mattered. By the time we turned on the spigot,
the smoke had increased twofold. This was a job for
professionals.

While I watched the fire from the junkman's yard,
Umberto came running down the hill. He was holding
a brown paper sack. The kind they gave out at the
corner store.

"What happened?" he asked breathlessly.

I shrugged. "Where's your brother?"

Umberto's face stretched in panic. "He's still in
there!" He dropped his sack and several cellophaned
candies rolled onto the pavement. "He's still in
there!"

"ALFONSO!" we screamed in unison at the burning
house. "ALFONSO!"

Behind us, a crowd was forming.

"Alfonso's still inside," we told each newcomer.

"Somebody's gotta save him!"

"ALFONSO!"

The crowd joined in. We were a chorus of house-
wives, grandmas and snot-nosed street rats. There
was nothing any of us could do but yell his name
and watch the cloud of smoke get bigger as the flames
peeked through the curtains.

"ALFONSO!"

The junkman was telling everybody the fire department was on the way. "I called them a good five minutes ago. I don't know what's taking them so long."

He was the only voice of authority until a red
pick-up screeched to a halt and a stranger got out.

"I saw the smoke from the freeway," the man said.

"We got a boy trapped inside," one of the ladies
told him.

"It's his brother." I motioned to Umberto, whose
face was molded into a silent scream.

"Don't worry, son," the man said. "We'll get your
brother out."

We watched with anticipation as he rushed into the
yard and tried the front door. The heat pushed
him back. He went down the side of the house, toward
the back, but that's where the inferno was strongest.
After realizing there was nothing he could do, the
man returned to the crowd, helpless like the rest
of us.

The junkman told him that he'd called the fire
department. "They'll get here when they get around
to it, I reckon." He snorted in disgust. "I pay my
taxes on time, least they can do is show up when we
need them."

In the distance, we heard the wail of a siren.
A murmur rose up in the crowd. We stared down the
street and cheered when the trucks careened around
the corner. As the firemen filed out, everybody
shouted at once, "A boy's still in the house!"

"Save the boy!"

Within seconds, the hose was attached to the hydrant
and a stream of water arched onto the roof of the
house.

There was less talk among the crowd while we watched
the firemen work. Two firefighters with axes smashed
the side windows and flames poured out like angry
old maids, shaking their fists at hooligans. It took
a second engine and two more hoses to get the blaze
under control, but the suspense remained palpable
until somebody called out, "Look! It's the boy!"

"They got him!"

We pushed closer to the action to see for ourselves.
A fireman emerged from the rubble with a bundle in
his arms. It was Alfonso. He was wrapped in a blanket.
I pressed against the chainlink and saw his face.
His skin was all black. Like a coal miner at the end
of a shift. The fireman carried him to the paramedics.
They strapped a mask over his face and laid his body
on a gurney in the back of an ambulance.

"Is he okay?"

"Can you tell if he's breathing?"

Before any of us could ascertain his condition,
the ambulance sped away. After that, we all watched
the fireman make sure the blaze was extinguished,
too stunned by what we'd just witnessed to go back
to our lives just yet. Although it felt like an
eternity, only fifteen minutes or so had passed
since the fire started. The adults were busy replay-
ing all the events with snippets of commentary,
asking each other questions not one of them could
answer. Even us kids knew this was a moment of
doubt and confusion. It changed everything. I was
afraid to look in Umberto's direction. Afraid of
what I'd see in his eyes. He was standing forlorn
near his fence when a woman charged through the
crowd and grabbed him by the collar.

"Que paso?" Her eyes were frantic.. She looked at
the house in ruins, then at the spectators in the
street and then at the firemen dragging a smoldering
couch onto the yard. She absorbed the scene as if
she were taking in a panorama. "Que paso?"
Umberto crumbled in her grip.
She shook his shoulder. "Donde esta Alfonso?"
Umberto looked at her like she was Medusa.
"Donde esta Alfonso?"
The fire chief approached and asked if she was
the mother.
"Donde esta mi nino?" She ran through the gate,
screaming at the men holding her back. "Mi nino!
Mi nino!"
Mrs. Garcia and a few other ladies went to calm
her down. Whispering in their secret tongue, they
coaxed her back through the gate and into a para-
medic truck with Umberto. As it pulled away, I saw
Umberto look back at the house, his face twisted in
anguish behind the glass.
"That boy's gonna be alright," the junkman said
assuredly. "They'll save him. The things they can
do with medicine these days..."
Others nodded and voiced agreement. But what did
they know? Alfonso died before the ambulance even
got to the hospital.

A few days after the fire, some of us went into
the burned out house to look around. We examined the
charred remains of furniture, clothes, toys and
appliances. We were shocked that some things had
escaped the inferno completely. A few dishes, still
clean enough to eat off. A couple photographs only
slightly singed along the edges. In Alfonso's bedroom
the walls were like tar. Except for one spot in the
corner. We stood in silence, knowing that's where
they found his body. Then one of the guys said what
we were all thinking, "That Alfie... man, he was a
major pyro."

Mister Fancy Pants

It was a Friday night when Royce barged through the front door and said, "Saddle up, boys."

We gathered around the kitchen table, where Royce sat unfolding a paper triangle, and watched him tap a small mound of white powder onto a vanity mirror.

"Who's ready to put some hair on their chest?" he asked.

"Me! Me! Me!" I shouted. I'd seen enough after-school specials to know I wanted in on this action.

"What's this look like, a fucking candy store?" Royce rolled a five dollar bill into a straw and snorted one of the lines he'd formed with a razor blade. He passed the mirror to Mark, who followed his brother's lead. Then the set-up went to Frankie. I was next in line, writhing with anticipation. But when I reached for the rolled-up bill, Royce halted the progression.

"Aren't you a little young for this shit?"

"Yeah, right." I tried to snatch the mirror. "I want my share."

Royce jabbed his finger at me. "Don't make me spank you."

"Oh, no! Grandpa's gonna get the paddle," I said in mock terror.

"Let him try a little," Mark said, his voice congested. "Give him half a line."

"Fuck that! I'll take half now and the other half right after that."

"Not with that attitude you won't."

"Fuck you! Gimme my share!"

"How old are you anyway? Ten? Eleven?"

"Fourteen." I rounded up.

"Hell, when I was your age, I was already in juvie. You ever been to juvie?"

"Nah. They gave me probation instead."

"Oh yeah?" Royce seemed surprised. "What'd you do?"

"Got busted. Duh! Now let me try!"

Royce belly-laughed and handed me the mirror. "You're alright, kid. You got balls. And that's more than I can say for these two butt-buddies." He smacked Mark in the head and socked Frankie in the shoulder with a left and a right. They were too glassy-eyed to even flinch.

"Watch out, dude." Mark flipped his hair back in place. "Royce might try to make out with you. All that time in the can, he's probably gone queer."

I stuck the bill into a nostril and leaned forward. The powdery blast hit me like the first rush of a roller coaster. Minus the butterflies.

"Your parents better not find out about this," warned Royce. "I don't wanna get the law on me just so you can feel bigtime."

"My folks don't give a shit what I do." I wiped my nose and resisted the urge to sneeze. "They're too busy with their own problems."

"Still. Keep your trap shut. Got me?"

I zipped my lips and threw away the key. "Mum's the word, kimo sabe."

"I'm serious."

I pointed at my lips and mumbled.

30

For the next half hour we sat around the living room talking shit while Mark worked the stereo. He was playing a Boston tape as if he were manning the space shuttle, hitting the stop button midway through a song, fast-forwarding to another, adjusting the EQ and repositioning the speakers.

"Stop tweaking on that shit, dude!" Frankie shouted over More Than A Feeling. "Just play the damn tape!"

"Fuck off!" Mark growled. "It's almost perfect."

We continued listening to the same three songs over and over until Sandy showed up. She walked through the door like a tickertape parade in a tube-top and skin-tight Sergio Valentes. "What're you homos up to?"

"I'll show you a homo!" Frankie stuck out his tongue and wiggled it at her.

"You wish." Sandy flipped him off and sat down at the table. She saw the mirror and smiled at Royce. "Chop chop!"

"Where's Paco?" Royce asked as he arranged a line for his sister.

"His name is Es-te-ban." She emphasized each syllable. "He's Spanish. Not like the wetback whores you fuck."

Royce handed her the mirror. "Okay, how's Es-te-ban?"

"Driving me nuts like always." She snorted loudly and pinched her nose. "He keeps following me around like a puppy. He's out there, right now."

"Where?"

"Outside."

"Outside here?"

"Yeah. Goddamn, you're an idiot." Sandy went to the window and pulled the curtain aside. "See?"

Across the street, a tall guy stood on the side-walk, looking back at us.

"He ran all the way from momma's house," she said. "Even though I told him to stay put."

"Maybe he's checking on his property," suggested Royce.

"Oh, that bike's mine. I don't understand half of what he says, but I'll swear on a stack that he gave me that moped. He's lucky I let him use it to go to work." Back at the table, she went in for another line.

"I wasn't talking about the moped."

"Fuck you!" she snapped, her voice high-pitched as she clamped her nose between her fingers. "He don't own me. I can do what I want."

"Bullshit. If a guy gives you something, he damn sure ain't giving it up for free. Face it, sis. Your ass belongs to Paco, long as it's glued to the seat of his bike."

"Oh yeah? Watch this." Sandy grabbed my wrist. "Come with me."

I followed her to the porch. She put her arms around my neck, glanced at her boyfriend across the street, and kissed me. Long and hard. I knew she was only trying to make a point, but I didn't care. I pawed at her tits as she sucked my neck. Then, just when things were getting hot and heavy, she pushed me away and went back inside. Dizzy from lust and excitement, I stumbled after her, trying to cop a feel.

Sandy slapped my hand. "Stop! You got all you're gonna get!"

"Ah, c'mon," I pleaded. "Don't be such a tease."

"No." Sandy walked to the table and sat down next to her brother.

"Don't torture the poor kid," Royce said. "Take him in the bedroom and make a man outa him."

"Like he would know what to do." Mark guffawed.

"Fuck you. I been with tons of chicks."

"Yeah, Sally, Sue, Betty, Veronica and Mary," Frankie said, counting his fingers.

"Does your mother count?"

"Watch it or I'll kick your virgin ass."

"Whatever. I ain't no virgin."

Sandy looked up from the mirror. "That's too bad. I mighta fucked you if you was."

"Really? I am a virgin. I am!"

"But you just said you had all this experience."

"I was lying."

"Shocker of the century!" Mark and Frankie cracked up.

Sandy smiled. "Why should I bust your cherry if you gonna lie to me? That ain't cool, man."

"I'm sorry," I said earnestly. "I won't do it again."

"Too late, pee wee."

I shrugged and went to the bathroom to check out
the small hickey forming on my neck. It stung like
hell, but I pinched the pink bruise to make sure
it came in good.

Later that night, after Esteban gave up his vigil
and left the moped parked in the driveway, we were
hanging out on the porch drinking Budweisers. Royce
let me join in, even though I was spilling more beer
than I was drinking. I'd cajoled another line of
coke and the world was spinning so fast I went into
hyper-gear to keep up.
   "Check out my new threads!" I shouted as I began
runway modeling the black jeans and striped button-
up my old man had bought me the previous weekend
when I went to visit him at his apartment. It had
been ages since I'd been shopping for new clothes.
The rest of my wardrobe was threadbare and frayed,
and last year's sneakers slapped against the ground
when I walked.
   "Look at mister fancy pants," cooed Sandy, egging
me on.
   "You're one slap-happy son of a bitch!" Royce
shook his head and chuckled into his beer can.
   While I was demonstrating how good my ass looked in
the new jeans, Mark shoved me into the overgrown
bushes that lined the porch.
   "Hey, asshole!" I crawled out of the briars and
brushed the cobwebs and plant fragments off. "These
clothes cost more than your fucking life, you rotten
bastard."
   Mark reared up, but Frankie held him back. "Hold
up, man. I just thought of something..."
   Mark smirked. "You thinking what I'm thinking?"
   "Pants him!"
   The cheer went up and I stared at them in dis-
belief.
   "C'mon, dudes. That's so lame."
   I looked to Royce and Sandy for support, but they
were too busy laughing. By the time I thought to run,
Mark and Frankie had my shirt in their fists. As I
struggled to escape, the buttons went, Pop! Pop! Pop!
   "Fuckers, my shirt!" I flailed my arms to break
free. In the process, the fabric ripped and the
shirt was torn off my back.

"Mega, dude!" Mark and Frankie tossed the rag back and forth, laughing. "Mega!"

"I can't believe you just did that!" I started back to the porch, thinking play-time was over, but they were just starting to have fun.

Mark and Frankie came at me with malicious intent. They grabbed my arms and swung me onto the grass. I stumbled before I could run.

"Motherfuckers!" I screamed. "Stop!" As I tried to fend them off, I looked at the porch. Royce and Sandy were laughing and shouting advice.

"Hold his arms!"

"Get his legs!"

Mark and Frankie lifted me off the ground. I saw the sky and their maniacal grins, then the ground. Then the sky again.

"One!"

"Two!"

"Three!"

I hit the turf head first with a white light thud. Mark still had me by the feet, holding me upside down.

"MOTHERFUCKERS!"

Mark and Frankie each took a pantleg and yanked furiously while I struggled to kick free, digging my fingers into the grass, clutching for ballast.

"Turn him over!"

Despite my epileptic fit, they got me onto my stomach. Frankie sat on my back and pinned my arms. Defenseless, I felt my pants slide down my legs.

"Get off me! Motherfuckers!" I croaked, out of breath from Frankie's weight. With my face in the grass, all I heard was laughter.

"Now let's make sure he's really a boy!"

I felt their hands on my boxers.

"NO! NO! NO! NO!"

I managed to bend my legs, but they dragged me across the yard until the seams split.

"Nuclear wedgie!"

"Mega, dude! Mega!" Mark roared as Frankie waved his trophy in the air.

I lay on the ground with my hands cupped over my crotch, feeling the sharp blades of grass poking my exposed flesh. "You guys SUCK! FUCK YOU!"

On the porch, Royce and Sandy were laughing so hard they had to hold each other up to keep from falling.

"Is that a toothpick between his legs?"

"He's got balls like little peanuts."

I grabbed my pants and the remnants of my shirt and took off down the street. In a neighbor's yard, I got dressed. The fly on my jeans was busted during the melee and wouldn't fasten properly. I started walking, holding up my pants with one hand and my shirt closed with the other.

I'd made it a few blocks when I heard the whine of a moped approaching. I was about to cut through somebody's yard, but I heard Sandy's voice. She was alone.

"Get on. I'll take you home."

I didn't respond, just kept walking. Every muscle in my face was clenched to hold back the waterworks.

"C'mon! They were just fucking around. You know how they get."

She was riding alongside me slowly.

I started walking faster.

"Don't be a baby! Get on the bike!"

At the intersection, I turned the corner and ran.

"Fine! Be that way!" Sandy yelled after me. She revved the engine and peeled out.

A Note on the Type

Like all previous issues of Piltdownlad, this was
typed on an Olympia manual. My machine is an instr-
ument. The stories I compose on it mere ren-
ditions. As I type, I get lost in the flow, the
rhythm of the keys, and this guides me through the
process. The composition. I know there are going to
be inconsistencies, flubs and mistakes. The process
lends itself to errors, misstrikes, etc. And once
I pull the sheet from the roller, the performance
is over. The page is scanned and manipulated on the
computer, though I only make changes to the text
when necessary. I stick to copyediting and not a
second rendition. What's come out is out. /It should
also be noted that, as is the case with all the stories I print in this zine, there has been some creative
engineering to maintain the narrative and dialogue
that may or may not be accurate to flesh out the
characters. A lot of it fairly accurate. To the best
of my memory. Some parts might have happened differ-
ently than what I've recorded, depending on whom
you ask, but as far as I can know the truth and per-
ceive reality, to the best of my ability, this is
how it went down. So my use of a term like "creative
engineering" is not meant to cause confusion, more-
over, it's to cover my ass if anybody wants to take
me to task for honest reportage. It begs the question,
can we ever know the truth? Is anything true? Or is
it all perception and prejudice?

PILTDOWNLAD

A PERSONAL NARRATIVE ZINE

AVAILABLE TITLES

Piltdownlad #6: INSTITUTIONALIZED - An exploration of abuse told from the perspectives of the abused and the abusers. "A powerful, humanizing work." - Broken Pencil 100pp./5.5"x8.5"/perfect bound $6.00

Piltdownlad #7: THE MURKY REALM - A biographical sketch of an improbable union... the story of how my folks got together, fell apart, came back together just to fall apart again. "...meticulously crafted and thoroughly fascinating..." - One Minute Zine Reviews 44pp./5.5"x7"/ $3.00

Piltdownlad #8: PAMPHLETERIA: The Rise and Fall of Phony Lid - Adventures in the publishing underground. The first of a proposed three part series on how I started a publishing company in the kitchen of the only house in an Alabama trailer park. 64pp./5.5"x8.5" perfect bound $5.00

Piltdownlad #8.5: THE CULT OF TEDDY RUXPIN - How I lost religion, discovered punk and made true friends after moving to small town Alabama. 40pp./4.25"x5.5" $2.00

A MASQUE OF INFAMY - My autobiographical novel about moving from LA to small town Alabama in the 80s, discovering punk rock, rebelling against the rednecks and bible-thumpers, dealing with an abusive home life and ending up in a mental hospital. "... twists the horror of growing up in a highly dysfunctional family into a hilarious tale of survival." --Lydia Lunch 320pp./5"x8" $14.00

All prices postpaid in US.

To order, send cash, money order or trade to:
Kelly Dessaint, Po Box 22974, Oakland, CA 94609
Order online through kellydessaint.com.

KEEP PRINT ALIVE!